SHADOWS OF THE HEART

Lorena McCourtney

Curley Publishing, Inc.

South Yarmouth, Ma.

Library of Congress Cataloging-in-Publication Data available

Published in Large Print by arrangement with Donald MacCampbell, Inc. in the United States, Canada, the U.K. and British Commonwealth and the rest of the world market.

Distributed in Great Britain, Ireland and the Commonwealth by CHIVERS PRESS LIMITED, Bath BA2 3AX, England.

Printed in Great Britain

SHADOWS OF THE HEART

Chapter One

The San José sunlight was blindingly bright as Trish Bellingham stepped off the plane. Mountains soared in the distance, mist-shrouded tops looming regally above cloaks of incredibly green vegetation – vegetation that thrived on soil made rich and fertile by the same volcanic ash that in ages past had rained down destruction. Trish found the vividly illustrated paradox a little breathtaking, somehow unexpectedly inspirational, but then she realized that the other tourists found her blocking their way. She smiled apologetically and hurried into the modern terminal building.

The formalities with Costa Rican officials took only a few minutes. Trish spotted Edith before the other woman saw her. It was Edith, wasn't it? Trish paused, mentally trying to project into the present that old photograph of the half-sister she had never met.

The woman turned and looked at Trish. She had dark brown hair, fine dark eyes. She was prettier than the plain, unsmiling girl in the photograph. No, perhaps not prettier, Trish decided, cocking her head thoughtfully.

1

Handsome. A handsome woman, her hair done up in a regal coil of braids, tall, with the defiantly proud posture of a woman who knows conventional beauty is not one of her assets. The young woman took a tentative step toward Trish.

"Trish?"

"Edith?"

Impulsively Trish threw her arms around Edith and hugged her enthusiastically. She felt Edith stiffen and she stepped back and smiled awkwardly. "I'm sorry. I – I guess back home we're just a hugging family."

"I know," Edith said softly, her dark eyes suddenly, unexpectedly bright with a hint of tears. "I remember."

Trish caught her breath with the sudden realization that, of course, Edith would remember. How old was she when the breakup occurred? Five? Six?

Edith reached out and took Trish's hand in hers. "You look so much like I remember our mother. I used to brush her hair and wish that mine were as pretty and golden. And she was so petite and slim. Like you."

Trish laughed, feeling oddly uncomfortable with Edith's obviously painful memories. "She still is, though now it takes a couple of weeks each year at some expensive health spa to keep her that way."

2

"Edith?"

Both young women glanced up at the sound of the male voice, Trish startled, Edith apologetic. Edith smiled and tucked a hand under the man's arm to draw him closer.

"This is Armando Albéniz," she said proudly. "My fiancé." Edith's face changed, subtly softening as she looked at the dark-haired, handsome young man at her side. Now she really was pretty, Trish decided. There was a light about her face, almost a glow. Trish had heard love could do that for some women, but she had never seen such visible proof of it until this moment.

"Armando," Trish repeated warmly. "I'm so pleased to meet you."

His smile flashed and he dipped his head in acknowledgment of the introduction. "You have made us both very happy by coming for our wedding." His English was excellent, with only a trace of an accent.

"I hope I'll be of some help and not just get in the way," Trish said.

"I would be happy if we would just do it simply and do it now," Armando said. He rolled his eyes in mock exasperation. "But women . . . they must fuss with dresses and veils and flowers and food. Three months yet to wait," he groaned.

3

Edith laughed, obviously delighted with his mild teasing. "Trish, are you hungry? Let's have lunch before we drive back to the *cafetal*."

Cafetal. Coffee plantation, Trish translated slowly, still a little awed that she had actually come. She usually did not do things so impulsively. Then she realized they were waiting for her reply.

"I'm starving," she said honestly.

Armando gathered up her luggage and led the way to a sleek Mercedes parked outside. Trish tried to see everything on the drive through the city streets, but that was impossible. She found herself mostly surprised that San José was such a bustling, energetic city, not at all slow and sleepy as she had expected.

The restaurant was dim and cool, a relief after the dazzling brightness and noise outside. Armando recommended the seafood and Trish had a delicious shrimp salad, exotic with a mixture of tropical fruits. The talk was light, drifting from subject to subject with ease: the college she had been attending, the current coffee harvest on the *cafetal*, wedding preparations, a new horse added to the stable, the food. Finally Trish leaned back, blissfully full and relaxed.

"Would a cigarette be out of order? I

4

don't smoke much, but after such a meal —"
She glanced around, seeing only one other
woman, obviously a tourist, smoking.

Armando laughed and produced both a
cigarette and a flick of his lighter. "We expect
anything of you American women."

The remark was made laughingly, without
malice, and Trish accepted it in the light
vein in which it was offered. She leaned
back, savoring the coffee and cigarette, letting
Armando and Edith's conversation, now in
soft Spanish, drift by her pleasantly.

But then she became aware of something
less pleasant, a distinctly uncomfortable
feeling that someone was watching her.
She straightened up and looked around
tentatively, finding herself staring directly
into the intent, dark eyes of a man sitting a few
tables away. He made no effort to look away
or to pretend he had not been watching her,
and Trish's eyes uneasily broke the contact
first. There was nothing bold or flirtatious
in the man's steady gaze. Trish was not
unaccustomed to that flirtatious sort of look
and would have known how to handle it, but
this was different, and there was something
disconcerting in this dark, almost brooding
inspection.

Finally she leaned forward uncomfortably.
"Do you know that man over there in the

corner? He keeps looking this way."

Edith was prevented from seeing the man by an obstructing support column, and Armando had to turn and deliberately look. The man in the corner gave Armando a cool nod of recognition, and Armando returned it with equal coolness.

"Our neighbor," he said. There was a totally different tone in his voice now: almost a curl of the lip. "Señor Marcantonio de la Barca himself."

Trish, puzzled by the change in Armando, glanced at Edith. Edith shrugged. "It's an old story," she said. "I'll tell you about it some other time."

The chance meeting seemed to have shattered the pleasant atmosphere, and Armando stubbed out his cigarette. "We should be going. I'm sure Trish would like to have some rest."

That was true. She had spent most of the night on the plane and then had an uncomfortable layover in Mexico City at an hour when there was little to do but sit and wait. But the lunch had been so pleasant and agreeable that she hated to see it end on this rather unpleasant note.

"Is he alone?" Edith asked curiously.

Armando did not turn to look, but Trish did cautiously. "No, there is a woman with

6

him." Trish hadn't noticed her before, so disturbing had she found the man's gaze. Now the woman, whose back had been turned to Trish, shifted slightly and Trish saw her face in profile. She was a beautiful woman, with creamy skin, gleaming black hair caught up with a jeweled comb, and eyes with just a hint of an almond shape. Even in a roomful of attractive Costa Rican women she stood out, her beauty more vivid and dramatic than the others. "She's very lovely," Trish said.

"It must be Ramona de Cordoba. I heard he was seeing her. She's a very well-known singer here in San José."

As if to confirm that comment, the American woman who had been smoking suddenly went over and asked for her autograph. Armando stood up, rather abruptly signifying the meal had come to an end. Trish could still feel the man's eyes on them as they left the restaurant.

Outside, the unsettling vibrations created by Marcantonio de la Barca's presence lingered, and Armando was silent as they left the city and headed for the coffee country to the north. Edith talked sporadically, drawing Trish's attention to points of interest, though her words were mixed with occasional anxious glances at Armando. Trish was interested in the sights, of course, but weariness from the

7

activities of the last few hectic days was beginning to catch up with her.

She leaned back, wondering what her parents were going to say when they learned she had abruptly dropped out of college and gone to Costa Rica. Trish had never been quite able to understand her mother's seeming indifference toward Edith, the child from her first marriage. That indifference seemed even more puzzling now that she realized Edith's memory of their mother was of an affectionate, hugging person. And yet, Trish reflected, that contradictory part of her mother's nature was evident even in her treatment of Trish herself. Her mother was affectionate, bubbling, and loving when she was around, true, but Trish's actual upbringing had been left mostly to her grandparents in Minnesota, while her parents chased around the world on business and social pursuits.

Trish and Edith had carried on a rather stilted, pen-pal correspondence while Trish was in grade school, but since then the contact had dwindled to the occasional birthday card. Then, completely out of the blue, had come Edith's letter inviting . . . no, more than inviting, almost begging . . . Trish to come and stay for Edith's wedding to Armando Albéniz, manager of the coffee plantation. It was an important time of life, a time when a woman needed family around, Edith had said, and Trish was all she had.

The letter had come at a propitious moment in Trish's life. The quarter was ending at college. She had no real thoughts about dropping out, but she had no real desire to continue either. She felt as if she were drifting aimlessly, without a goal. She had many interests in life but none that seemed compelling enough to pursue deeply. Spending the next few months in Costa Rica suddenly seemed like a marvelous idea. It would enable her to get to know the half-sister she had never met and also get a long-distance perspective on her life and what she wanted to do with it.

Trish dozed, vaguely conscious of passing through a medium-sized town and some small villages, but not really wide awake until they started up the rougher, winding road that led to the *cafetal*. Here the incredible green that she had seen on the mountain slopes from a distance was all around them. The road twisted again and she had a breathtaking view of the volcanic mountain whose shoulders they were traversing like insignificant insects creeping around on a giant. The green vegetation became sparse near the top then yielded to barren, lifeless rock, as ominous

9

and alien as a part of some dead planet.

"What is that?" Trish gasped. "I mean, is it an active volcano?"

Edith laughed and shook her head. "No, you needn't worry. It won't send rivers of lava pouring down on us in the middle of the night – though Marcantonio de la Barca says his grandfather could remember steam escaping from it when he was a boy." She hesitated. "And I suppose its name might hint that it is not as sleepy as it appears."

"What is its name?"

"Monte Decepción."

Mount Deception. Oh, yes, Trish thought with a little shiver, that name could be significant. Somewhere back in time the mountain had evidently done something to earn that ominous title. Another twist in the road and they were in the shadow of the towering mountain.

"But Edith is right about the lava," Armando added reassuringly. "Our Costa Rican volcanos are of the ash-producing variety, which is not to say, of course, that they cannot be extremely dangerous. But you don't need to worry about Decepción."

"There is an interesting place we'll have to show you though," Edith said. "Quite unusual because, as Armando says, these are ash-producing volcanos. But sometime long

10

ago lava evidently escaped from a fissure near the base and formed huge, hollow underground tubes."

This bit of information earned Edith a narrow, disapproving scowl from Armando, which puzzled Trish at first until Edith went on hurriedly.

"My father was always convinced there should be early Indian artifacts in or around these tubes and caverns, and he used to spend hours poking around there, though he never found anything. I used to go along and scare myself silly peering into those eerie tubes. A little like peeking through your fingers at a horror movie, I suppose." Edith laughed, though she sounded a little uncertain and Armando did not join in.

No doubt the possibility of artifacts was what disturbed Armando, Trish thought. As a native Costa Rican, he probably would not approve of an American making off with native artifacts, even as long-term a resident as Edith's father had been.

They rounded another curve and there was the house. Trish caught her breath in sheer delight at its loveliness. The house had two stories in back, with rambling wings surrounding a central courtyard. The roof was red tile and there was an iron-grilled balcony overlooking the courtyard. Lush bougainvillea tumbled everywhere, shadowing the windows, draping the deeply overhanging verandas.

A servant came and collected Trish's baggage, evidently already having been instructed as to which room she would occupy. Armando excused himself to take care of some business, suggesting Trish have a good nap before dinner, to which she readily agreed. Edith accompanied her directly to the room and Trish had only a vague impression of wood-beamed ceilings and richly appointed rooms in the other parts of the house.

Trish was quite delighted with the pleasant little room and adjoining bath to which Edith showed her. There was colorful handmade furniture that Trish recognized as probably having come from the famous oxcart-making area of Sarchi. She went to the window and pulled back the filmy curtain. She had expected to see a shady courtyard and instead was surprised to see a modern swimming pool.

"When my father's health started to fail, the doctors told him a daily swim might do him good, so we had the pool installed," Edith explained. "He still tries to swim occasionally, but –"

"You mean he is still alive?" Trish turned away from the window, surprised. Then she apologized. "I'm sorry. I didn't mean that

12

the way it sounded. It's just that I assumed you wouldn't have invited me if he were still alive."

Edith smiled. "I love my father and we still have long talks. But somehow, at the time of a marriage, it is not the same as having another girl, a woman relative around."

"I can understand that," Trish said quickly. "It's just that ... I mean, under the circumstances ..." Her voice trailed off doubtfully.

Edith nodded. "Yes, I know. And that is why I hope you will understand when I do not introduce you to my father. He has never forgiven my ... our ... mother for the way she left him for another man. And you, as the daughter of that other man ..." She lifted her eyebrows slightly, questioningly, lowering them when Trish nodded in understanding. "I'm sure you can appreciate that in his present physical and mental condition the shock of meeting you might be very bad for him, especially since you do resemble our mother so much."

"He has ... mental problems?" Trish asked tentatively.

Edith hesitated. "Bitterness takes many unpleasant forms," she said enigmatically. "His mind wanders. But he stays mostly in his room and has a private nurse, so there

13

is little danger that you will run into him. And if you should accidentally meet him –" She broke off, hesitated again, frowned. "I think it would be best, of course, if you do not reveal to him who you are and get away as quickly as possible."

Trish nodded. "Of course. I'd never want to do anything to upset him." She hesitated, tempted to ask more about that curious meeting at the restaurant with the cold, aloof neighbor, but she decided that this was not the time. For a moment she tried to bring his face back into focus, but she could not. Those dark, intense eyes had dominated everything about him, though she had a vague impression that he had been handsome in a lean-faced, aristocratic way.

Edith left then and Trish undressed and relaxed on the comfortable bed. The room seemed a little stuffy and she slid the window open to let in a breath of fresh air. There was a slight breeze that ruffled the filmy curtains and Trish dropped into a restful sleep almost immediately.

She woke sometime later, not certain how long she had slept but feeling much more relaxed and refreshed. Edith had not said what time dinner would be served nor how formal the attire would be. After some minor mental debate with herself, Trish opted for comfortable tangerine pants and a sleeveless white blouse. She was eager to get out and look around and did not want to be encumbered with dressy dinner clothes.

She wandered down the long, cool hallway, not seeing anyone until she found a side door that opened into the courtyard. The pool was clean and shimmering, with a cluster of lounge chairs at one end. Trish debated about changing into a bikini and taking a dip, but she decided that could wait. She was too eager to see everything now. She let herself out the iron-grilled gate and wandered around, inspecting the unfamiliar blooms and shrubbery. She had no idea what a coffee tree or bush or whatever they were looked like, but it appeared the commercially cultivated areas must be some distance from the house.

Then a high-pitched whinny attracted her attention. Horses? Yes, of course. She remembered Armando saying something about adding a new horse to the stable. She hurried around the corner of the house and delightedly headed toward the sound of the whinny. As a child in Minnesota, horses had been her frequent companions, but she hadn't been near a horse since high school.

She could see glimpses of neat white fences through the trees and the occasional flash of a chestnut or bay coat gleaming in the setting sun. There must be an easier way to get to the stables, she thought, as she struggled through the grass and underbrush. Obviously this was not the usual way, but finally she broke into the fenced clearing. The mares and foals looked up in mild surprise at her approach and then resumed their contented grazing, except for one bright-eyed filly that advanced curiously and then, with a flick of her heels, retreated to the safety of the mare's side. Trish laughed delightedly.

She wandered around, surprised to see so many apparently well-bred animals. Armando had casually mentioned a stable but this was obviously a well-kept breeding establishment as well. Then she heard again the excited whinny that had first attracted her attention and realized it came from a paddock set off by itself a little distance away. A magnificent chestnut stallion thundered along the high wooden fence, whirled, shook his head in equine anger, and stormed back to the far side of the paddock. His attention was on a mare a few fences away, who was watching his performance with interest.

Trish approached closely, curious and a little awed by the lithe, gleaming animal so different from the docile creatures she had ridden bareback in her childhood days. She peered through the boards and then climbed

16

to the top of the wooden fence to get a better view, slinging one leg over the top board for balance.

The stallion whinnied again, earning a soft reply from the mare, and his frustration increased. He galloped along the well-worn path beside the fence and then, for the first time, he spotted Trish. He faced her from across the paddock, ears alert, eyes intent.

"Come here, boy," she coaxed. "I didn't bring a lump of sugar, but I promise I will next time."

She broke off, astonished, as the alert ears suddenly flattened against the sleek head and the horse charged across the paddock, pure fury in every line of his gleaming body. He slid to a stop in front of her, one foot pawing the ground angrily.

"There, there, it's okay, fellow," Trish soothed shakily. The horses she had known had never behaved like this. Carefully, never taking her eyes off the unpredictable animal, she drew her leg back over the fence, and just in time because, without warning, the big horse suddenly reared, his forefeet slashing the air where her leg had been only moments before.

She clung to the fence, feeling it shake as the horse's hooves hit the ground and rose again.

"What the hell are you doing up there? Get down!"

Trish's already shaky grip on the fence loosened when she heard the angry, commanding shout, and she tumbled to the ground. Somehow one foot caught between the boards and she hung there, trapped, while the stallion plummeted up and down and wood splintered as his flashing hooves connected with the board fence.

"Demonio! Back! Get back!"

The horse retreated, still shaking his head angrily, and Trish looked up into the no less angry face of Marcantonio de la Barca. He stood there with hands on lean hips, feet spread arrogantly, his height and breadth of shoulder distorted and emphasized to a frightening degree by Trish's awkward position on the ground. He wore a white shirt, open at the throat, tan pants, and gleaming riding boots. His hair was as black as that of his female companion at the restaurant, his complexion smoothly tan both by sun and heritage. His eyes, broodingly suspicious of her earlier, flashed with fiery anger now.

"What are you doing here?" he demanded.

Trish, thoroughly frightened at first by the unexpected behavior of the stallion and this man's angry shout, was beginning to get a little angry herself. Whatever she had

18

done scarcely warranted letting her dangle there by one foot until she came up with some acceptable explanation. Her ankle was beginning to hurt too, bent at an awkward angle as it was. She twisted to a sitting position, trying to relieve the pain and free the foot, determined not to ask him for assistance.

Finally, scowling, he bent over and with a quick touch of capable hands released her imprisoned foot. She rubbed it, trying to revive the circulation, keeping her eyes on him as warily as she had the angry stallion.

"I ask you again, what are you doing here?" he said arrogantly.

"And I might ask the same thing," Trish retorted. "What are you doing here?" She couldn't possibly make her voice as arrogant as his, but she made it as icily aloof as possible.

"I happen to be here to supervise the breeding of my stallion to one of my more temperamental mares," he said coolly.

"These are your horses?" Trish asked, dismayed. "But I thought ... I mean, Armando mentioned a stable."

Marcantonio de la Barca looked down his aristocratic nose at her. "Armando keeps a few riding horses," he said, dismissing the stable with a negligent shrug. "The quality has decreased since he took over management

19

from Señor Hepler."

Trish scrambled to her feet, realizing she had evidently made a thoroughly gauche mistake in wandering onto the property of this neighbor, with whom relations were obviously already strained for some unknown reason. "I suppose I must apologize," she said reluctantly. "Edith and Armando told me you were their neighbor, but I didn't realize you lived so close. I knew the place has hundreds of acres and I thought the house was probably in the middle . . ." Her voice trailed off uncertainly under his unrelenting gaze and he offered no acceptance of her apology. A bit belligerently she added, "You must mistreat your horses or they wouldn't act that way."

"Demonio is, as his name indicates, something of a devil," Marcantonio de la Barca said calmly. "I can assure you that he is very well treated indeed. However, as I'm sure you'll understand, his disposition may be under some strain during the periods of breeding. In addition, he has always exhibited a certain contempt for women."

"Perhaps learned from his master?" Trish snapped.

His lips tightened momentarily but he merely shrugged again and said, "Perhaps." He gave Trish a thorough up-and-down look of appraisal that brought a flush of color to her cheeks, and there was a hint of wicked amusement in his voice when he added, "But that does not prevent either of us from being properly appreciative of female grace and beauty and its . . . ah . . . inherent usefulness."

Trish gasped, but he merely flashed a smile.

"What I mean, of course, is, where would we be without the beauty of women to brighten our homes and offices and beaches?"

Trish was reasonably certain that was not what he had meant, and she had a pretty good idea what he considered a woman's usefulness, but this was a subject she certainly did not care to pursue.

"It would seem to me," she said coldly, "that if you have a dangerous horse on the place, it would be wise to post signs to that effect."

"My people know of my stallion's disposition, and we do not generally have people from the Hepler property carelessly wandering over this way."

Trish glanced back the way she had come, realizing now why there had been no trail or path. It also appeared she would have to battle her way back through that underbrush, since she certainly would not ask this arrogant man for permission to cross his property and take

21

some easier way around.

"If you'll excuse me then, I'll just get back to the house," she said with all the haughtiness she could muster. "I'm probably late for dinner already."

She took one step and the foot crumpled beneath her.

Chapter Two

Again Trish lay inelegantly on the ground, Marcantonio de la Barca's powerful figure towering over her. They stared at each other, eyes locked, neither of them moving, and suddenly, unexplainably, Trish was no longer just humiliated and angry. She was frightened by this dark-haired stranger, as dangerous and unpredictable as the stallion he possessed. She scrambled toward the underbrush, but her awkward progress was no match for his lithe stride.

Unexpectedly he leaned over her and jerked her around by the shoulders to face him. "Who the hell are you anyway?" he demanded roughly. "What are you doing here?"

The sharp retort died on Trish's bloodless lips. "I . . . I'm Trish . . . Patricia Bellingham.

Edith Hepler is my half-sister. We've never met before, and she invited me to come down from the States to get acquainted and help her with her wedding plans and arrangements and then stay for the wedding." The words tumbled out of their own accord with Trish scarcely thinking what she was saying, unable to stop the flood of words even if she had tried.

His look was still calculating, but the steely grip on her shoulders relaxed slightly. "Have you sprained your ankle?"

Trish pulled back out of his grasp, her eyes still watching him warily. "I don't think so. I just twisted my foot."

"We'd better have a look and see. María up at the house used to take care of all my cuts and bruises when I was a boy."

Before Trish even had time to protest, he reached out and scooped her up in his arms. For a moment she was too shocked to protest, even after it had happened. Then she struggled wildly in his arms. "Put me down! Put me down now!" she insisted.

"Oh, no, Señorita Bellingham. I have no intention of letting one of you sue-crazy Americans drag me through court saying you were injured and disabled for life on my property." He looked down at her struggling figure, smiled slightly, and calmly tightened

23

his grip so she could scarcely move.

"I have no intention of suing you! And, as a matter of fact, I did get injured on your property. I could have gotten killed by your crazy horse or by your yelling and scaring me half to death!"

The storm of words brought no response from Marcantonio de la Barca, and in utter frustration Trish pounded on his chest with her closed fists. It had no more effect than pounding on a stone wall. Suddenly, instead of twisting and turning in his arms, she jerked her body straight and flat, almost hitting him in the face. The movement caught him by surprise and he stumbled forward, tumbling both of them to the ground.

But he didn't let go and his body was half over hers as they struggled on the ground. She rolled from side to side, brought her knees up and tried to shove him away, elbowed him in the throat. But she was no match for his greater weight and strength, and in moments she was pinned to the ground, panting. One of his powerful hands held both of hers over her head and her body was trapped beneath his.

She had only one weapon left and she started to use it, sinking her teeth into the flesh of his arm. But then their eyes met and there was a dancing light in his, and in furious dismay Trish realized he was enjoying this! She further realized that she had no idea what else he might decide to do, that they were alone and out of sight, and that even if she screamed, the inhabitants of the coffee plantation would probably not interfere in their *patrón's* activities.

Carefully she released the grip of her teeth on his arm. "Well?" she said icily, as if this were merely some sort of awkward situation.

"If you think you are ready now, Señorita Bellingham, we will go to see María," he said mockingly.

She didn't reply, and he cautiously released her hands, separated his body from hers, and gathered her up in his arms again. She didn't resist this time, simply lay there passively and regarded the whole situation with remote detachment, her arms folded against her chest. They moved toward the house in silence, his lithe stride not even slowed by her weight in his arms.

In spite of her determination to remain coolly detached, she was too curious not to twist her head and inspect the house as they approached. It appeared to be very similar to Edith's house, though it was hard to tell for certain, since they were approaching from the rear. It did have the same two stories in back, she was certain, plus the

25

rambling wings attached at right angles. It was probably older, she decided, though that was difficult to tell for certain with the lush drape of bougainvillea covering everything.

He carried her through a garden and to a back door where an elderly woman rushed out to meet them with an excited torrent of Spanish that went far beyond Trish's limited comprehension of the language. But the woman's genuine concern was obvious and she led the way through the house, past a dining room with heavy, ornate furnishings, to a comfortable sofa. She motioned to Marcantonio de la Barca to set Trish there. He explained the problem in Spanish to María.

"Really, this isn't necessary," Trish protested. "I just twisted my foot a little. I'm sure I can walk on it now."

He smiled faintly. "You are in María's hands now. You had better do as she says."

The woman was already bustling around, tsk-tsking over Trish's flimsy sandals, running gentle, capable hands over the tender foot. Shortly she disappeared and in a moment returned with towels and a basin of cold water. She wrapped the foot in cold compresses, which Trish grudgingly admitted to Marcantonio de la Barca felt very soothing. Darkness was almost upon them and he switched on several soft lamps.

The room was large, with a wooden-beamed ceiling, and enormous fireplace, and an abundance of lush indoor plants. The floor was tile, warmed and softened by colorful throw rugs. Trish wondered if the courtyard in this house also contained a swimming pool or if it were of the more conventional variety. María disappeared again, and Trish eyed her tormentor/benefactor warily. He offered her a cigarette, lit it for her when she nodded, then lit one for himself. He blew smoke lazily, his eyes following the blue drift.

"I take it you and the Heplers don't get along," she said tentatively.

He shrugged. "Robert Hepler is a fine man. When his health was better, we cooperated in many ways in growing and marketing our crops." He paused. "Armando is competent and efficient as a manager. And ambitious."

"He seems very deeply in love with my half-sister," Trish commented defensively. "And she is certainly madly in love with him."

He shrugged again. "They plan to be married," he said without interest, as if neither love nor marriage were of particular concern to him. He turned from the window where he was standing and unexpectedly added, "Did you know Armando before you came down here?"

27

"Of course not," Trish said, puzzled. She raised herself up on one elbow to look at him. "What in the world would make you think that?"

Again the negligent shrug. "Armando spent some time up in the States before he came to manage the Hepler *cafetal*."

Silence again. Marcantonio de la Barca did not seem to feel it necessary to fill silences with polite small talk. Finally Trish could stand it no longer.

"What do people call you?" she burst out curiously. "I mean, somehow I can't imagine that beautiful woman in the restaurant saying, 'Marcantonio, my dear, would you pass the salt, please?' "

He walked over to her and looked down at her, smiling faintly. "Women have called me many things," he said softly.

"I'm sure that's true. I was thinking of a few choice names for you myself today," Trish said tartly. "Though I suppose you are referring to more . . . ah . . . intimate terms of endearment."

Their eyes met again, but his were in shadow and she could not read their expression. He turned away and said briskly, "My fellow students at the university in the States also seemed to have trouble with my name. They shortened it to Marc. I suppose

28

that is as good as anything."

"You went to a university in the States?" Trish asked, surprised. "Which one?"

"Princeton."

Trish would have liked to ask more questions, but María bustled back then, bringing a soothing salve to apply to Trish's foot and ankle. A few minutes later, when Trish stood up, she found there was only a slight tenderness and she was quite able to walk. She thanked María with rather awkward Spanish.

"And thank you too," she said to Marc, unable to keep from adding under her breath, *I suppose*, since she still felt the whole situation was mostly his fault. "I'd better get back to Edith's. She'll be wondering what happened to me."

"I'll drive you," Marc said decisively. "You'll never be able to find your way in the dark now."

Trish started to protest, but realized he was correct, and remained silent. As they drove away from the house she could see the lights from Edith's house glimmering faintly through the trees. The drive seemed a long way around, past what appeared to be warehouses of some sort, and then back up to the Hepler house. Without waiting to see whether or not Marc would open the

29

car door, Trish jumped out the moment the car stopped.

"Thank you for the ride," she said a little breathlessly. The night was surprisingly cool and she shivered. "Well, good night."

He was still regarding her thoughtfully. "When you see Robert Hepler, you might tell him my offer is still open," he called after her.

"Offer?" Trish repeated doubtfully.

"He'll know what I'm talking about."

"*Your offer, señor, is no more welcome now than it has ever been!*"

The sharp words came out of the darkness of the veranda and Trish whirled, startled. Armando walked out, his posture rigid with anger. Someone from inside switched on an outdoor light and Trish could see the set expression on his face, the angry flare of his nostrils as he approached the car.

"And what, may I ask, are you doing on this property?" he demanded of Marc.

"It's my fault, Armando," Trish said hurriedly. "I wandered onto his property by mistake and —" She broke off and shot a glance at Marc's face hidden in the shadows of the car. "And I accidentally twisted my foot and he gave me a lift back."

Armando bent his head in a none too gracious gesture of thanks toward Marcantonio de la Barca. Trish had a pretty

30

good idea he was just as displeased with her for causing this awkward situation as he was with Marc for coming onto the property. She apologized profusely as Armando opened the heavy carved wooden door to the house. He continued to frown and Trish rattled on until finally he seemed to accept her apologetic babblings.

"There is much you do not know," he said finally, still disapproving. "Perhaps Edith would care to explain. I'm sure you would like to freshen up before dinner, however."

Trish agreed and practically raced down the hall to her room. She quickly washed up, applied a light touch of makeup, and slipped into a draped dress of silky nylon jersey in a pink that flattered her blond coloring. She was hungry, she realized, but she was almost as anxious to get to the dinner table to hear what Edith might have to say as she was to eat.

It wasn't until she made her way back through the main living room to the dining room that she stopped short in a rather startling discovery. The two houses were not merely similar in construction; they were exact duplicates of each other, or at least as much of them as she had seen – the same beamed ceilings, same size and shape, and arrangement of the rooms, same tile floors, same massive fireplace. The furnishings were different, of course, the Hepler house reflecting Edith's feminine touch, but the basic layout was the same. How peculiar.

Edith was already in the dining room fussing with wineglasses when Trish arrived. Trish apologized again.

"It's not your fault," Edith said quickly. "I should have told you where the property line is. I just didn't realize you would be up and wandering around so quickly."

"I guess I'm the curious type, but it's not a mistake I'll make again," Trish admitted, thinking of her almost violent encounter with Marcantonio de la Barca.

She hoped Edith would explain whatever there was to explain immediately, but Armando came in then and seemed to have dismissed the incident completely. He was jovial and pleasant at dinner, affectionate with Edith, bringing more than one flush of pleasure to her face. The food was marvelous: a flaky, tender fish, fresh vegetables, and the best coffee Trish had ever tasted, which seemed fitting here in coffee country. Over the fresh fruit compote for dessert Trish finally could hold her curiosity no longer.

"Would it be prying if I asked for a little more explanation of the situation with Marcantonio de la Barca? she asked

32

tentatively. "I don't want to make any more embarrassing blunders."

Edith sighed. "It's something that goes back a long way, something that we weren't even a part of in the beginning, and it should have been settled long ago."

"There is no way it can be settled now," Armando interjected grimly.

"You see, at one time years ago, this was all one large *cafetal*. There was just the one house then, the one Marc now lives in," Edith began. "Marc's grandfather owned it all. Then he died and his two sons operated the place together. But then they both fell in love with the same girl and the cooperation changed to jealousy and hatred. The girl married the older son, Victoriano. The younger son, Jacinto, was furious. Insanely jealous. Vindictive. They split the property in two pieces then. Jacinto got this half and for some reason known only to himself built this house as an exact duplicate of the other place. Perhaps he thought to entice the woman he loved to it in some way. Who knows? She never came, of course, and Jacinto never married. Then Marc was born and I guess that really set Jacinto off. He swore neither his brother nor his brother's offspring, Marc, would ever get this half of the place. In fact, he became almost obsessed with that fear.

33

He was so afraid he would die and Marc would somehow get the property anyway that eventually he sold it to my father. At a very bargain price, I must add," Edith admitted, "or we would never have been able to buy it."

"But I don't understand the enmity," Trish said slowly. Her wineglass was empty and Armando leaned over and refilled it. She declined his offer of a cigarette. "I mean, it isn't your fault Jacinto sold the place to you. Surely Marc can't blame you."

"That would be true if Marcantonio de la Barca were a reasonable man," Armando said grimly. "Unfortunately he appears to have inherited his uncle's predilection for strange obsessions."

Trish lifted her eyebrows. "Obsessions?"

"One obsession," Edith corrected, sighing. "He has always wanted to see the property as one *cafetal* again, with himself as owner, of course."

"He would do anything, anything," Armando repeated emphatically, leaning forward to further emphasize the point, "to accomplish this. Behind that facade of aristocracy, that smooth surface of sophistication, he is utterly and totally ruthless. But he will not succeed," he said, leaning back and smiling grimly.

"Then the offer he mentioned had

something to do with this property?" Trish asked.

"An offer!" Armando spat out the word. "He had in mind stealing the place for a pittance from a sick old man and a helpless girl, after he couldn't marry his way into possessing it for free," he added contemptuously.

Trish looked at Edith. She was flushed, her eyes agitated.

Armando reached out and put a possessive arm around Edith's shoulders. "He was in love with Edith." His fingers played with the nape of her neck and his voice softened as he looked at her face turned toward him. "I cannot blame him for that, of course. But Edith would never have him, nor the others who desired her equally as much." He took a sip of wine and offered her one from the same glass.

Trish suddenly felt that she was intruding on something very private. She felt something else too. Envy, she decided guiltily. It would take the deepest of loves for a man to believe that plain Edith was the object of the powerful passions of a man like Marcantonio de la Barca, plus numerous others. Because Edith was plain, Trish admitted, if you took away the glow of love. But Armando saw her through his own eyes of love and believed

35

that any man who looked on her must feel the same tenderness and passion that he felt. But if Marc was as ruthless and obsessed as they said, and Trish could certainly believe that he was, she had no doubt but that he had tried to marry Edith to obtain the property that way. It was to Edith's credit and good sense that she hadn't been taken in.

Trish sighed inwardly. She had been the object of a fair amount of male attention in her twenty years of life, but none to match Armando's feelings for Edith.

Armando glanced at Trish as if just then remembering that he and Edith were not alone. He removed his arm from Edith's shoulders. "Then, after Edith's father's health began to fail," he continued, "Marcantonio thought he had another chance. Edith could never manage the *cafetal* alone. Marcantonio ingratiated himself with Edith's father and began to make his offers." Armando's lip curled in a sneer. "At one time he almost had Edith's father convinced to sell, in fact. And Edith had so many problems running the *cafetal* almost alone that she was ready to let it go too."

"But that was when I found Armando," Edith interjected simply.

"And so now all of Marcantonio de la Barca's hopes and plans have been smashed and he's sulking," Trish mused. But the word did not fit Marc, of course, she realized. He might be furious. He might engage in ruthless action, violence even. But sulk in a corner? Never.

"So now you know all our little family skeletons," Edith laughed. "And Marc's too."

"Oh, I imagine he has more than anyone suspects," Trish observed, thinking of his references to the endearing names offered him by willing women.

"Well, enough of Marcantonio de la Barca," Armando said briskly. "Would you like some music, Trish?"

They went into the living room then and Armando played the guitar. Edith joined him in singing some of the Spanish songs, her voice husky and sweet. Trish listened until he swung into the lively strains of a tune with which she was familiar, "La Cucaracha." Then she joined in and they all wound up laughing and stomping in an impromptu dance.

Edith finally broke up the little party, her laughter ending almost abruptly. She said she must go and spend a few minutes with her father before bedtime. Trish and Armando had another glass of wine and talked about Edith and her marvelous good qualities, generally steering away from the subject of

Marcantonio de la Barca and his obsession. Armando was an entertaining host, amusing Trish with anecdotes about the *cafetal*, and describing interesting sights in Costa Rica that she might enjoy seeing.

When Trish finally went to her room, she was surprised to find how late it was. She wasn't tired or sleepy. The afternoon nap must have done it. She unpacked, shook the wrinkles out of her clothes, hung her dresses in the closet, and made neat piles of undies and sport clothes in the bureau drawers.

Still wide awake, she poked around looking for something to read but she didn't find anything. She took a leisurely bath, hoping that would make her sleepy, but that didn't work either, though it did ease the soreness from her twisted foot. Finally there was nothing else to do but go to bed. She had closed the heavy velvet drapes over the filmy curtains when she came into the room, and now she opened them again, deciding to open the window a crack for her usual nighttime whiff of fresh air. But now the window was stuck and wouldn't budge and she finally gave up on it, thinking she would have to ask Edith to get one of the servants to unstick it tomorrow.

When she lay down then, she was not only wide awake but the room felt closed-in and

38

stuffy besides. She got up, prowled around the room, stuck her nose out the hall door to see if the air was any fresher there, and tried the window again. Then, looking out at the pool, she had an inspiration. A midnight swim! Why not? She wouldn't bother anyone. No one would even know.

She quickly dug her blue-and-white bikini out of the drawer and slipped into the skimpy outfit. She wished she had brought her terry cloth beach cover-up, but she hadn't really thought there would be much opportunity for swimming, since the coffee plantation lay well inland from both of Costa Rica's coasts. She draped a towel around her shoulders and padded silently on bare feet down the dimly lit hall and out the door she had used earlier.

Another dim light burned somewhere in the rear of the two-story section of the house, but there was no sound of activity. The air at this high altitude was somewhat cool and she shivered as she crossed the cement walk bordering the pool and draped her towel over the arm of a lounge chair. By then she was covered with prickly goose bumps and the water felt warmer than the surrounding air to her testing foot.

She slipped silently into the water and sidestroked to the far end, her smooth strokes and underwater kicks barely rippling the surface. She swam underwater, her body warming with the invigorating movement, did a smooth underwater somersault, finally breaking to the surface with scarcely a splash. And then, in what seemed a perfect complement to an already magical scene, the moon peeked over the tile roof and sent a glitter of silver spinning across the water. She floated silently on her back, looking up at Monte Decepción and thinking that now even that towering monster seemed less threatening, more protective than ominous.

Her thoughts drifted back to Marcantonio de la Barca and some puzzling contradictions about him. He could probably be charming, she thought grudgingly, though he had not chosen to honor her with much of that facet of his character. Charming but arrogant, she decided. And ruthless. What would he do now that it was obvious he would never get this half of the plantation he so deeply coveted? Well, he could always console himself in the charms of that Ramona whatever-her-name-was, Trish sniffed to herself. The woman hadn't looked like the type who would enjoy wrestling matches on the ground, but you could never tell. Remembering the way he had held her down, the way their bodies had touched, and the wicked gleam in his eyes, she felt an unexpected warmth rising deep within her.

She did not pursue nor inspect that feeling. She pushed herself away from the wall of the pool with an energetic shove and swam rapidly to the far end with an efficient crawl, not bothering to maintain silence. Then, the burst of energy gone, as well as that disquieting warmth inside her, she floated on her back again.

And then, in the same unpleasant way that it had happened in the restaurant, she became aware that someone was watching her. She tried to tell herself that was ridiculous. You couldn't actually feel someone watching you. Eyes didn't send out vibrations.

Yet the feeling persisted. She put a hand on the edge of the pool and rested, her eyes searching along the rows of blank windows on either side and to the rear of the house, lifting to the second story, darting around to inspect the iron gate. She saw no sign of movement, heard nothing, and yet the feeling intensified.

The air was motionless, the only sound the faint barking of dogs in the village some distance away. Nothing out of the ordinary, nothing threatening, and yet suddenly Trish shivered almost violently. She was merely getting chilled from the cold air and water, she tried to tell herself reassuringly, but

41

she knew that wasn't true. The tremor of her body came from a puzzling fear and apprehension, the almost uncanny feeling that the invisible eyes watched her with evil intent.

Swiftly she pulled her slim body out of the water, drying herself hurriedly as she walked to the door, suddenly anxious to be back in the security of her own room. Her wet feet left dark imprints on the concrete, like some presence following behind her from which she could not escape. She swung the heavy door open and gasped as she caught a glimpse of shadowy movement. She slapped a hand over her mouth to stifle a scream, trying not to panic. It wasn't movement, just a shadow caused by the closing door . . . wasn't it?

The door closed, and still the shadow moved again. It was a man, tall but with narrow, drooping shoulders. Trish could see him in silhouette, his long arms dangling, his large hands opening and closing convulsively. Trish stood frozen, like some wild creature caught in a blinding beam of light. He took a step toward her, lifted one hand.

"Carole," he breathed. "Carole Ann!"

Carole Ann . . . her mother's name!

Trish took a step backward, her breathing fast and shallow. This must be Robert Hepler then, Edith's father. Another step, another hoarse whisper. Trish looked around wildly.

The hallway to her left, to her room and safety, was between her and the man. She edged along the wall, her hands behind her feeling the way, her eyes never leaving the menacing figure. His head turned slightly, following her movement, and she saw gray hair, uncombed, shadowy eye sockets, a caricature of a nose. She almost screamed, but she gritted her teeth, sensing that a scream, a noise, anything, might galvanize those groping hands into action.

Then she felt it, the end of the wall, the corner turning into the other hallway. With one last terrified look at the man she turned and fled, racing down the hall with pounding feet, not knowing if he was inches behind her. Her panicked flight took her beyond her door, all the way to the darkened living room, and she hid there, panting, her heart throbbing through her body, until she dared peer down the hallway again.

It was empty. Cautiously, alternately looking before and then behind her, she made her way back to her room. By then she was shivering, her teeth chattering. Somewhere she had lost the towel, evidently near the door when she first encountered the man, because she did not see it in the hallway.

She opened the bedroom door, and started to flick on the light but decided against it.

43

She felt around for a lock on the door but found only an old-fashioned keyhole that required a key she did not have. She fumbled around the darkened room, searching for something to brace against the door, trying to remember what furniture the room contained, but everything was solid, heavy, almost unmovable. Finally she pulled the only thing she could move, her luggage, and piled it against the door. The slight protection was not reassuring.

She slipped into bed without even removing the damp bikini and, in a sitting position, pulled the covers up around her neck, her eyes fastened on the door. She couldn't actually see the door in the dark room, but any movement to open it would reveal a crack of light that she would be able to see.

She sat there tensely, her heart and mind racing. Edith had suggested that if she accidentally ran into Robert Hepler, she get away as quickly as possible. Trish had interpreted this to mean merely the avoidance of an unpleasant scene that might upset a sick man. But maybe it was more than that. Maybe Edith had been subtly warning her that the man was dangerous, that his bitterness toward her mother had been even worse than that, Trish thought shakily. Robert Hepler thought she was the woman who had betrayed and abandoned him, the woman he hated.

Trish's eyes ached with the intensity of staring into the darkness, and occasionally she glanced through the filmy curtains at the courtyard pool outside. The scene was sharp with contrasts, pitch-black shadows along the far wall, moon-silvered water, the walkway as bright as day. Trish thought she would never sleep and certainly did not intend to let her vigilant watch slip into unwary slumber.

But sleep she did, restlessly jerking awake once to find her neck cramped and stiff, half-waking another time to move away from the damp spot left in the bed by the bikini. She dreamed strange, frightening, disconnected sequences, hands reaching, groping for her, choking tighter and tighter around her throat. . . .

She woke gasping and choking. She lay back dizzily, trying to dispell the frightening dream, only to feel acrid smoke clog her nose, throat, and lungs. She coughed and gasped, felt her senses reel dizzily and realized that she was close to being overcome by the smoke, close to unconsciousness. She flung her arms out, groping for the bedside lamp, and dimly felt it crash to the floor.

She floundered out of bed, stumbling in the tangle of sheets and blankets. Smoke, smoke everywhere. No flame, just that acrid,

45

choking smoke, but her lungs felt as if they were on fire. Her chest heaved, fighting for oxygen that was not there. The smoke was so thick, she almost seemed to claw her way through it.

The door . . . the door . . . she must get to the door. She had to clutch the bed to keep her balance. Her lungs were bursting. She stumbled over scattered luggage . . . fumbled desperately for the door . . . clutched the doorknob with failing strength.

She turned the doorknob. Nothing happened. She tried again. Still nothing. And then in pure panic she frantically pulled, yanked, twisted.

The door was locked.

Chapter Three

Trish staggered away from the door, one hand clutching at her throat. Strange lights danced in front of her eyes, so many lights and yet she could see nothing. Her mind reeled dizzily. She felt as if she had been running, running until her lungs were bursting and her throat parched in pain, running for her life. But now she could go no farther.

Her foot struck a suitcase and she stumbled to her knees, her mind barely registering the new pain. Her hand touched something hard.

The lamp. She was so close now to being overcome by the smoke that even as she struggled to her feet with the lamp in one hand she had only a vague notion of what she should do with it.

The window. It was a lighter oblong against the blackness of the wall. Or was the lighter shape only another of the geometric lights that danced in her eyes? Irrationally, her mind wandered. She remembered the way she amused herself long ago as a child in the darkness, squeezing her eyes shut tightly and watching the shapes play against her eyelids. . . . No, she must not think about that now. There was something she must do.

It seemed to take more strength than she possessed, but some instinct for survival forced her to act. She swung the lamp at the oblong, heard the tinkle of breaking glass. The sound, distant though it seemed, encouraged her, and she swung again and again as the life-giving air surged around her. Finally she dropped the lamp and leaned weakly against the nightstand, gulping fresh air. She felt it clearing her lungs and mind, felt the strength returning to her healthy young body. She wiped at her watering, burning eyes, relief washing over her, but when she opened her eyes, there was new terror.

The rush of fresh air had fanned the smoldering mattress into flame. In another moment the filmy curtains would catch. Trish screamed wordless sounds of pure terror. She grabbed a pillow and beat at the flames but they spurted higher, dancing demons that nipped at her hands and hair.

She wasn't even aware that the door had opened until she heard shouts in Spanish amd someone took the pillow from her. A moment later water streamed through the smashed window and the flames died with a protesting hiss. A spray of water hit Trish and she covered her face with her hands.

"*Señorita! Señorita*, you are hurt?"

Trish blinked. Someone had turned on the overhead lights, but the room was still hazy blue with smoke. The smell of soggy bedding mixed with the acrid odor of the burned mattress. The servant who had spoken helped Trish sit in a heavy wooden chair. A sharp order in Spanish cut off the deluge of water spurting through the window. Trish opened her mouth to speak, but only a hoarse croak escaped.

"Trish! My God, what happened?" It was Edith, her long dark hair hanging in a single braid down her back. Her astonished eyes took in the condition of the room, Trish's disheveled appearance, and her incongruous bikini attire.

Trish cleared her throat and finally managed to speak. "I don't know what happened. I went for a swim –" She broke off, her mind, even in this groggy condition, hesitating about telling Edith in front of the servants of that frightening encounter with Edith's father. "When I came back, I fell asleep and when I woke up, the room was filled with smoke. I tried to get out, but the door was locked."

"Locked!" Edith exclaimed. She turned to the middle-aged servant and spoke to her in rapid Spanish.

Trish was too weary and confused to translate the reply but there was no mistaking the vehement shake of the woman's head. She even made motions in the air to illustrate how quickly and easily the door had opened. Trish stared at her in bewilderment.

"But I'm sure it was locked. I was trapped or I wouldn't have smashed the window!" The exclamation left Trish gasping for breath and she went into a spasm of coughing.

Edith patted her back. "You must try to keep calm. Perhaps you were simply too frightened to think clearly. This was formerly my room and I remember that the door would

49

stick sometimes," she added soothingly.

"And the window was stuck too," Trish remembered suddenly. She stood up, startled to find how unsteady she was on her feet, but she managed to make the few steps to the window. "This afternoon the window opened easily but tonight it was stuck tight, just as if someone had . . ."

Trish's voice trailed off as she and Edith inspected the window together. Trish's blows with the lamp, weak though they had seemed at the time, had been strong enough to damage the window frame as well as shatter the glass. It was impossible to determine now what condition the frame had been in before Trish battered it.

"You're shivering," Edith said suddenly, her voice concerned. "We'll talk about this in the morning. What you need right now is a warm bed. I'll take you to another room."

Edith found Trish's blue robe in the closet and was just helping her into it when Armando appeared in the doorway. He was scowling, still tightening the rope belt of a corduroy robe around his waist. His dark hair was slightly awry, as if he had hurriedly smoothed it back with his hands after leaping out of bed.

"Trish!" He muttered an oath in Spanish. He grabbed her by the shoulders and then

50

stepped back to inspect her singed hair and disheveled condition. "What have we done, bringing you here and letting this happen to you!"

He snapped an order in Spanish and the middle-aged woman hurried to the door.

"I was just going to take Trish to another room," Edith explained.

"But how did all this happen?" Armando demanded. He took a long stride toward the soggy mattress and bent to retrieve something. "You were smoking in bed."

"Oh, no," Trish said. She shook her head. "I rarely ever do that, and I'm sure last night I didn't."

She broke off suddenly as Armando held up between thumb and forefinger a bare half-inch of cigarette stub.

"You see, you must have set the cigarette here," he said, pointing to a small burn on the nightstand. "Then you fell asleep and the cigarette either fell or you knocked it to the bed, where it set the mattress to smoldering."

Trish looked at the cigarette stub uncertainly. She hadn't been smoking before she fell asleep . . . or had she? She remembered huddling apprehensively in the bed, watching the door until her eyes ached. She couldn't remember lighting a cigarette, but it was quite possible she had done so, she

51

supposed. Obviously she had. The proof was right there in Armando's hand.

She shook her head, feeling disoriented and dazed. "I must apologize. Ruining this lovely room, disturbing everyone . . ."

The servant reappeared with a silver tray holding a bottle and glasses. She offered them to Armando.

"Ah, this is what we all need," he said. "Brandy."

Trish shook her head, but Armando insisted she take a few sips. The liquid felt fiery as she swallowed it and she was again conscious of the raw soreness of her throat. But the bracing, strengthening liquid seemed to help dissolve the blue haze that had enveloped her mind as well as the room.

She hadn't been smoking in bed. She was sure of that. And the door had been locked, not merely stuck. But that didn't make any sense, she thought, bewildered. Unless . . . The apparition of Robert Hepler rose in her mind, the lanky hands opening and closing convulsively.

"There, you're shivering again," Edith scolded gently. "Come with me."

Trish returned her glass to the tray and thanked Armando. Edith put an arm around Trish's shoulders to steady her as they walked down the hall and around the corner to another room. Trish apprehensively wondered where Robert Hepler's quarters were located. Edith efficiently threw back the bedcovers, fluffed the pillows, and pulled the drapes. Trish perched on the edge of the bed, but, weary as she was, she couldn't force herself to relax.

"Stay with me a few minutes," Trish said. She smiled self-consciously. "I don't feel like being alone just yet."

"You need your rest," Edith protested. "After such an unfortunate and upsetting accident –"

"Edith, something else happened tonight that I think you should know about." Quickly Trish told Edith about the hallway encounter with her father earlier that evening. "I know seeing me must have upset him terribly. In fact, he seemed to think I was our mother. He called me Carole Ann."

"Did you have any further conversation with him?" Edith asked.

Trish shook her head. A slight frown creased Edith's smooth forehead, but she put a reassuring hand on Trish's shoulder.

"Don't worry about upsetting him. By morning he may forget he even saw you," Edith said. "But I'll check with his nurse. If he really seems disturbed, she can give him something."

Trish hardly knew how to put her awful suspicions into words. "But suppose he . . . I mean . . ." she began awkwardly.

There was an odd look on Edith's face. "What is it you're trying to say?"

What was she trying to say? That Robert Hepler had crept into her room and left a lighted cigarette with the deliberate intent of burning her to death?

Carefully, trying to keep her voice from shaking, Trish said, "I felt someone watching me while I was swimming. If . . . if as you say your father has had mental problems, and you mentioned his bitterness toward Mother . . ."

"You think my father tried to kill you? That he deliberately . . ." Edith's face paled visibly and her voice trailed off as she stared in horror at Trish.

The suspicion seemed even more terrible now that it lay exposed between them in blunt words.

"Maybe not deliberately. Or maybe not me. I mean, if he thought I was our mother." Trish stammered. "Oh, I don't know what I mean! But I'm sure, almost sure, I wasn't smoking, and the door was locked."

"Trish, you're not going to go away because of this, are you?" Edith knelt by Trish's bed, her hands reaching for Trish's, her voice anxious. "You mustn't. Not after all these years, just when I need you so much."

The thought of leaving had not entered Trish's mind and she was touched by Edith's concern. "Of course I'm not leaving," she said quickly. "I wouldn't miss your wedding for anything."

"I'll make sure that my father has no opportunity to leave his room unattended again," Edith added, her voice almost grim.

Trish noted that Edith, after her initial shock at Trish's suspicions, did not deny the possibility of their being true.

"You must not let this frighten you away," Edith repeated.

Trish squeezed Edith's hand reassuringly. "I won't." She shrugged and smiled. "And perhaps it was just an accident. Maybe I was smoking in bed. Everything will probably look different in the daylight."

Edith stood up. "I'm sure it will. But if you'd like me to post one of the servants as a guard by your door . . ."

"No, that won't be necessary," Trish said quickly.

Edith gave her another reassuring smile as she closed the door. Trish's eyes lingered on the knob. It had a privacy lock, the kind where you simply pressed a small button in the center of the knob to lock it. Was that what had happened? Had she in her panic

55

simply locked herself in that other room?

The thought was momentarily reassuring, but then she remembered. The lock on that other room was not of this type. It required a key. But Edith had said the door tended to stick occasionally, and that was surely the rational explanation. She had fallen asleep while smoking in bed and then in panic had mistaken a door that was merely stuck for one that was locked.

Now she got up, went to the door, and firmly pushed the button. It was time to get what sleep she could in what remained of this shattered night.

She slipped the silky robe off, then realized she had no nightgown. She thought about going back to her former room to get one, but she abandoned that idea immediately. No more traipsing around tonight. She quickly stepped out of the bikini and slid naked between the smooth sheets. The sensation was pleasing, momentary coolness giving way to delicious warmth against her skin as she drifted into a dreamless sleep.

When she woke, she was temporarily disoriented both in time and place. With the heavy drapes drawn the room was still in almost total darkness, but a crack of light along the edge revealed bright daylight outside. Trish's chest felt tight and scratchy inside, and a tentative deep breath brought a twinge of pain. Then she became aware of a light tapping on the door.

"Trish? Trish, are you all right?"

Trish had to try twice before she could make her voice respond. She cleared her throat and managed to say hoarsely, "Just a minute. I'll unlock the door."

She slipped the blue robe on. Every muscle felt sore as she hobbled to the door. Edith stepped inside, looking concerned. She was wearing a white dress, almost like a nurse's uniform.

"I hated to disturb you, but I was getting worried."

"It must be late." Trish's voice was a croaking, foreign-sounding noise.

"I'm going to bring the doctor over later today," Edith said firmly.

Trish started to protest, but talking was just too much of an effort. Unresisting, she let Edith help her back into bed.

"You just stay there," Edith instructed. "I'll have breakfast brought to you. We're lucky that today is the doctor's regular biweekly visit to the village. It's one of the services the *cafetal* provides to the workers. I usually go to the village and assist him. I'll bring him over as soon as he can get free."

Trish nodded, surprised to find how weak she was and how scratchy and raspy her breathing felt. Shortly after Edith left, a servant appeared with an attractive breakfast tray. The juice was particularly refreshing to her raw throat and Trish asked for more. The servant also brought a concoction that tasted a little like a homemade cough syrup Trish's grandmother used to give her. Somehow Trish doubted that it had any great medicinal value, but it felt soothing and she dozed off again after eating.

She awoke for the second time that day to hear a commotion from somewhere down the hallway. Suddenly the servant who had brought her breakfast appeared in the doorway.

"*Señorita,* you have a visitor," she announced breathlessly, disapproval quivering in her voice.

It must be the doctor Edith was sending over, Trish thought, though why that should arouse the servant's ire, she did not know. Then the servant stepped aside and another figure loomed in the doorway.

Marcantonio de la Barca!

Trish's heart pounded erratically in reaction to his totally unexpected appearance in her private bedroom. Tall, lithe, faintly predatory, he paused in the doorway.

58

Trish was so astonished that she couldn't have said anything even if her voice had been working properly. Now she understood the servant's agitation. A gentleman did not call on a lady in her bedroom. Or was it that Marcantonio did not call on anyone in this household?

"Marc. What a . . . a surprise!" Trish finally managed to croak weakly. She clutched her robe around her, glad she hadn't removed it after breakfast. She touched her tangled hair uneasily, feeling the stubby ends where the fire had singed it.

He strode into the room and looked down at her, his expression inscrutable, his dark eyes appraising. Trish somehow felt utterly exposed, utterly vulnerable under that superior gaze. Why had he come?

"Won't you sit down?" she said, motioning to the room's single chair.

She thought for a moment that he was going to refuse and retain his position of domineering superiority, gazing down at her, half-sitting, half-lying on the bed. But he finally turned and sat in the chair she indicated. She pushed herself into a more upright position, careful to keep the robe clutched around her. She wondered uncomfortably if he knew she wasn't wearing anything under it.

59

"I understand there was a fire," he said abruptly.

"More smoke than fire," Trish said. She rubbed her throat. "How did you know?"

He shrugged. "Things get around."

Trish quickly surmised that the servants of the *cafetals* were on good, gossipy terms, even if the *patrónes* were not.

"Young ladies should not smoke in bed," he added. He might not be physically towering over her now, but there was a certain patronizing superiority in his voice as he offered the advice.

"You certainly seem to know everything," Trish snapped. "I suppose you also know about my midnight swim first?"

His sensuous lips twitched slightly. "Perhaps." He glanced around the room. "I assume this is not where the fire occurred?"

"No, I was in a different room, one that looks out on the swimming pool." Her throat felt better now, not nearly so rough and scratchy. The syrupy medicine must have had some effect. There was a glass of juice on the nightstand and she took a sip.

"But you were smoking in bed?" he persisted. He raised a dark eyebrow. He was lounging back in the chair now, seemingly relaxed and carrying on a casual conversation. Yet Trish was reminded of a cat she had

60

once owned, a cat who would lie motionless, seemingly oblivious to the world, until some unwary bird came within striking distance. Then the cat struck with deadly accuracy. It was not a reassuring comparison.

Trish hesitated before answering his question. She hated to admit she had been smoking in bed and thus corroborate his obvious opinion of her as a careless, irresponsible little fool. But if she didn't admit to smoking in bed, she would have to offer some other explanation, and she certainly could not voice her suspicions about Edith's father to this man.

"I suppose so," she finally answered reluctantly. Something tickled in her throat and she coughed nervously.

"You were fortunate you were not seriously injured," he commented.

"Yes, I suppose so," Trish agreed. "I suppose if the curtains had caught fire, the entire room would have gone up in flames."

"It is also fortunate someone heard your cries of distress."

Why, Trish wondered, did she have the feeling, in spite of Marc's casual manner, that she was being interrogated? Marc seemed only mildly interested in her answers, lounging in the chair, watching her lazily through half-closed eyes. And yet she had the feeling

61

nothing escaped his attention. She nervously reached up to tuck a stray strand of hair behind her ear and realized his eyes had dropped to where her hand had been holding the robe together. Now the front of the robe gapped open, revealing the curving hollow between her breasts. She hastily clutched the clinging material together again. He smiled faintly, making her feel somehow prudish.

When she made no comment on what he had said, he prompted her with, "Someone did come to your aid, I take it. Or were you alone?"

"I managed to break the window and then the servants and Edith came." As an afterthought she added, "Of course I was alone. It was past midnight."

"And where was Armando during all this uproar?" he inquired dryly.

"I'm sure I don't know," Trish answered, beginning to feel irritated. She wasn't sure if she was irritated by his questions or by the way he seemed to appraise her, find her reasonably attractive, and then dismiss her. "Really, I'd rather not discuss the fire anymore. It was merely an unfortunate accident. So if you've found out everything you came for –"

"Forgive me," he said. He dipped his head in apology but there was something faintly

62

mocking in his tone. "We'll talk of other things. Have you met Edith's father yet?"

Trish bit her lip. Of all the subjects to pick for casual conversation, why did he have to pick that one? "No, we haven't been introduced yet," she said evasively.

"I see."

"Why did you come over here?" she blurted out suddenly. "You must know Armando will be furious if he finds out. And I can't really believe you're all that interested in the results of my . . . my smoking in bed."

He did not seem disturbed by her outburst. He regarded her thoughtfully, one lean, aristocratic hand tapping the little table by the window lightly. "Insofar as I know, Armando does not own the *cafetal*. At least not yet. Robert Hepler does. And Robert Hepler has never told me I am not welcome here."

His contemptuous opinion of Armando as some sort of pretentious upstart was obvious, but Trish was reminded of Armando's equally contemptuous remarks about Marc's attempts to ingratiate himself with Robert Hepler in order to buy the plantation cheaply.

"And as for why I came . . ." His smile was lazy, but something smoldered beneath it, and Trish's heart jumped wildly when he added softly, "Would it surprise you to know that I am interested in everything about you?"

The unexpected reply flustered Trish. She cleared her throat nervously, wondering if he was sincere or if this was some sort of game he was playing to amuse himself. She would not put it past him to come here for the sole purpose of infuriating Armando. She toyed uneasily with the drapery cord by her bed, realizing for the first time that Marc's house and stables were visible from this window.

Suddenly Marc leaned forward, his lazy manner gone, his dark eyes intent. A muscle twitched along his lean jaw. "Go home, Trish," he said harshly. "Go home before —"

Trish never knew whether it was his totally unexpected words or the intensity of his eyes or just the overwhelming nearness of him, but something within her reacted with a violent spasm of coughing. She gasped for breath and her eyes watered and her chest ached.

When she finally leaned forward weakly, her face in her hands, she was aware of some sort of commotion. A short, stocky man was waving his arms and chastising Marc in rapid Spanish. The servant woman had returned and was excitedly insisting that it was not her fault, that she had tried to keep Marc out. Edith wasn't saying anything, but her distress was obvious.

Only Marc was utterly calm, the eye in the center of the hurricane around him. He

64

was standing now, towering over the others, unperturbed. He looked toward Trish, his expression aloofly inscrutable.

"I am sorry if I disturbed you, *señorita*," he said. "I wish you a quick recovery from your unfortunate accident."

He strode toward the door without looking back, and the little doctor looked vaguely uncomfortable, as if suddenly thinking that perhaps he should have treated such a powerful person with greater courtesy. Then, shrugging, he turned his attention to Trish and proceeded to give her as thorough an examination as was possible with the limited equipment he had. He listened to her heart and lungs, inspected her throat, nose, and eyes, and tsk-tsked over her singed hair. He spoke little English, but his instructions concerning several days of bed rest were plain enough.

When the doctor was gone, Edith looked at Trish anxiously. "What in the world happened? Why did Marcantonio come here?"

Trish shook her head. She leaned back against the pillow weakly, her blond hair fanned out around her. She breathed carefully, trying to avoid that little ticklish feeling that would send her into another spasm of coughing.

"He asked about the fire, that was all."

"Armando will be furious if he finds out Marcantonio was here." Edith paced nervously between bed and doorway, as if half expecting Armando to come roaring down the hallway.

"That's what I told him," Trish agreed. "But he didn't seem worried about it."

Unexpectedly Edith smiled. "No, I don't suppose he would be." She sat on the edge of the bed. Her hair was done up in the regal coil of braids again, and she looked very much the proud *cafetal* owner. But it was somehow difficult for Trish to imagine that the aristocratic and sensuous Marcantonio de la Barca had ever been wildly in love with her.

"Armando is very jealous of . . ." Trish paused, searching for the right word. ". . . of Marc's former relationship with you, isn't he?"

Edith's smooth skin flushed slightly. She hesitated, playing nervously with the engagement ring on her left hand. "Marcantonio was never in love with me," she admitted self-consciously. "At one time I had a terrible crush on him, and I'm sure my father would have been delighted if something had come of it. But I am hardly Marcantonio's type of woman."

Edith smiled slightly at Trish's questioning look.

66

"Somehow Armando got the impression Marcantonio had been madly in love with me and I –" She flushed again and averted her head. "I let him believe it. To tell the truth, I have not had many suitors."

"I'm sure it has been difficult for you, living way out here with so many responsibilities and all. But now you have Armando, and I'm glad he seems to realize what a lucky man he is to have you." Trish smiled and reached over to squeeze Edith's hand warmly. "Besides, I don't see anything wrong with letting a man think he has a little competition to keep him on his toes."

"You're very understanding," Edith returned the squeeze. "But I think the matter of the supposed relationship between myself and Marcantonio is only a small part of the hostility Armando feels for him. It is perhaps that Marcantonio has always had so much, and Armando has had to work and struggle for everything."

"My grandfather always said it was better to work for something than have it handed to you on a silver plate," Trish commented. Somehow Trish found herself relieved to hear Edith's confession about the truth of her relationship with Marc. Intuitively Trish had known he had never been in love with plain, quiet Edith, and she thought more highly

67

of him, knowing he had not attempted to deceive Edith in this matter in order to get the *cafetal* he coveted. Was it even possible that his desire to reunite the two halves of the plantation was less of a ruthless obsession than Armando believed?

Edith's next words dispelled that thought.

"The other things Armando said are quite true, however," Edith went on in a low voice. "Marcantonio had tried, with many offers, to persuade my father to sell to him. He can be cruel . . . and ruthless. I'm sure there are many women who hoped to snare him into marriage who would attest to that."

"But there isn't much he can do about the *cafetal*, is there?" Trish argued lightly, ignoring the comment about Marc's prowess with women. "After all, your father has refused to sell, and Armando is here to manage the coffee business now. Someday, of course, I imagine it will belong to you and Armando together."

Edith nodded, but an unexpected turmoil in her fine, dark eyes startled Trish. "It would seem so, and yet . . ."

"Yet what?" Trish prodded.

Edith shrugged and stood up. "Marcantonio's uncle's obsessive fear forced him to sell the plantation in spite of his love for it. I do not know

68

to what extremes Marcantonio's obsession to possess it again might carry him."

Trish shivered as the calm words, unemotionally spoken, hung between them. Somehow Edith's quiet statement was more disturbing, more damning than Armando's passionate tirade against the man.

Trish bathed later in the day, trying to get rid of the smell of smoke that clung tenaciously to her skin and hair. The servants moved her clothes from the other room, but they also smelled of smoke and everything had to be taken away for laundering. Trish wrote a letter to her grandparents and another long one to her parents, though she left out any mention of the fire so as not to upset them even more than they would be when they found out she had dropped out of college.

Mostly she just stayed in bed, finding it not too difficult to follow the doctor's orders, since any exertion tended to bring on the racking coughs again. Her glance strayed frequently to the other house, partially visible through the trees, but there was no sign of Marc's coming or going from it.

Just as frequently her thoughts went back to the unexpected visit from Marc and the even more unexpected things he had said. One minute he had seemed to say he was interested

69

in her, and that smoldering glance had perhaps said more than words. Just thinking about it sent a shiver up Trish's spine.

But in the very next breath he had harshly advised her to go home. *Go home before –* Before what? Had he some suspicion that the fire in her room might not have been an accident? He had dealt with Robert Hepler in the past. He must know of his peculiarities. Was Marc warning her to leave because she was in danger from Edith's father? Marc had, she remembered, mentioned him only moments earlier. Trish hadn't let herself examine that night any further; hadn't let herself ask the questions that didn't fit in with the neat little smoking-in-bed explanation.

Deep down she had to admit that she was perhaps as much hurt as puzzled by Marc's harsh advice. Reluctant as she might be to confess it even to herself, considering the arrogant way he had treated her, Trish had to admit she was attracted to him. It was hardly flattering to have a man to whom she was attracted urge her to leave, not stay.

A servant brought dinner to Trish's room and Edith stopped by later in the evening. Edith had a slightly harried look. She said that Armando was "upset," which Trish took to be a polite term for a sullen, angry reaction to Marc's visit. Edith indicated there were

70

some problems at the *beneficio*, the coffee-processing plant, which had further upset him. In any case, he ignored Trish and did not make even a courtesy call to inquire how she was feeling.

The next morning Trish felt much improved. The scratchy rawness was gone from her throat and deep breathing brought no pain nor inclination to cough. She accepted a leisurely breakfast in bed, still watching out the window for Marc, but somehow knowing he was long since up and about the business of the coffee plantation. After breakfast she bathed and dressed in blue denim shorts and a comfortable halter top. There was no reason, she decided, that she could not do her lying around in the sun and at least have a tan to show for the time spent doing nothing. The laundered clothing smelled fresh and clean now, all trace of the smoke gone.

She poked around in the bureau drawers and bathroom cabinet where the servants had placed her things, looking for her suntan lotion, but she could not find it. She finally decided it must have been left in the other room.

The door to that room stood wide open as she approached, and from inside came voices and sounds of hammering. Trish peered inside. A woman was washing smoke

71

stains from the walls and two men were working on the smashed window. Trish exchanged smiling friendly greetings with them and finally located her suntan lotion in the bathroom.

She paused on her way out the door and glanced back, finding the terrifying experience that had happened here only two nights ago difficult to believe. Everything looked so ordinary. The heavy drapes had been taken down and bright light flooded the room now. The woman hummed as she worked and the men chattered cheerfully in Spanish. Only the bed looked odd, with an empty oblong hole where the burned mattress had been removed. There were some very mundane-looking dust balls on the tile beneath the bed.

Yes, her imagination had really been running away with her that night, she decided. Carelessly smoking in bed, stupidly panicking over a stuck door . . . That was the only sensible explanation.

Her hand dropped to the knob and slowly she pulled the door shut, opened and closed it again. It moved smoothly, without the slightest tendency to stick. Trish frowned, remembering how frantically she had jerked on it that night.

But the men had probably already repaired

the sticky door, she decided. She was just about to turn and leave when the door was opened from within the room.

"Ah, *señorita*," the woman who had been washing the walls exclaimed. "I leave the door open for air." She waved a hand in front of her nose to indicate distaste for the vague odor of smoke that still lingered.

Trish glanced at the other closed doors along the hallway and then impulsively pointed to the old-fashioned key-type lock on this one. "I was wondering . . . this seems to be the only door with a lock like this. Do you know why?"

The woman looked momentarily puzzled, then laughed. "Ah, I had almost forgotten. It was long ago, when the *señorita* was young. Señor Hepler could not bear to strike her when she was disobedient, and so he would lock her here in her room for punishment now and again. He would wave his arms and shout that she would stay there until she was sorry for what she had done." The woman's eyes twinkled. "But I do not think it was any great punishment because the *señorita* would lie on her bed and read and never say a word. And soon Señor Hepler would feel worse than she did and unlock the door."

The woman laughed gaily as if this bit of family history was very amusing, but Trish had to lean against the wall for support, the comfortable, sensible explanations for that night tumbling chaotically around her.

"And the . . . the key?" Trish added, almost in a whisper, her throat painfully dry.

"Ah, it has been so long, but . . ." The woman peered and pointed to a nail slanting into the door frame at chest height. An old-fashioned iron key dangled from a nail. "There it is. I remember once when Señor Hepler threatened to lock the *señorita* in her room for some reason. She marched right over there and reached up on her tiptoes and handed the key to him."

The woman laughed again in fond reminiscence as she went back to her scrubbing, but Trish just stood there, stunned, the bottle of suntan lotion clutched so tightly that her knuckles turned white.

Robert Hepler had used the lock on that door many times, had probably installed it for the specific purpose of disciplining Edith, since it was different from the other locks. There was no doubt in Trish's mind now that the door had been locked, not merely stuck that fateful night. Robert Hepler thought locking someone in a room was a suitable form of punishment.

Had he decreed a similar, only far more deadly, punishment for her?

74

Chapter Four

"Trish, what in the world have you been doing? You're not supposed to be up!" It was Edith, hurrying down the hall toward her.

Trish licked dry lips, her thoughts in turmoil. The fire had been no accident and the door had been locked. She was almost certain of that now. She kept seeing Robert Hepler as she had seen him that night, not the soft-hearted father the servant remembered, a father who hated to discipline an errant child. She saw a man bitter or mentally deranged enough to use any means of revenge against the woman he hated or the daughter of the man who had taken that woman from him. Or perhaps, in his mixed-up mind, they were one and the same person.

"Trish, are you all right?" Edith asked, her forehead creased with concern

"Yes, I'm fine. I – I was just looking for my suntan lotion."

"You should have sent one of the servants," Edith chided, but her mind was obviously on something else. "I was looking for you because I wanted to tell you Armando is going to join us for lunch. He's in a much better mood now," she added.

Edith's plain face looked alive and animated, reflecting how Armando's attitude could affect her. Trish made a quick decision. There was no point in bringing up the matter of the lock and key. Edith knew they were there and had tacitly admitted her father could have been responsible for the fire. But she had also been definite in her assurances that she would take measures to see he would not be a danger to Trish again. Determinedly Trish decided now to ignore all that had happened. She almost wished, in fact, that she had not stumbled onto the dismaying discovery about the lock and the easy availability of the key.

"Why don't we eat by the pool?" Trish suggested, forcing herself to reflect Edith's gay attitude.

"And later this afternoon the seamstress is coming with the material for my wedding gown." Edith sounded almost girlishly happy.

Trish and Edith were already waiting by the pool when Armando drove up in the Mercedes. Trish was still wearing her shorts and halter but Edith had on a skirt and longsleeved blouse, plus a floppy red straw hat to protect her face from the sun. Trish felt vaguely underdressed as Armando strode through the courtyard gates in a well-cut, lightweight suit.

"Ah, my two favorite ladies," he said, sounding as cheerful as he looked. He brushed Edith's cheek with a kiss and took a seat under the umbrella that shaded the luncheon table. "Trish, I must apologize to you," he said earnestly.

Trish murmured something noncommittal, relieved that Armando evidently did not intend to make an issue of that visit from Marc.

"No, I must apologize," he insisted. "We had some problems at the *beneficio* and I am afraid I took my annoyance out on you and Edith. I have not even been to see you since the night of that terrible accident. Are you recovering satisfactorily?" he added anxiously.

"Oh, yes," Trish assured him. With a laugh she added, "And I think it cured me of smoking in bed."

Armando laughed too. The servant brought lunch then and while they ate, Armando talked enthusiastically about the rising price of coffee and what a heavy harvest they were getting this year. Edith's eyes, full of adoration, hardly left his face. Finishing his meal, Armando leaned back, his eyes on Trish.

"But I'm sure you're not interested in

hearing me talk about business all the time, are you? You must find us very dull here."

"Trish gave me her word she would not leave before the wedding," Edith interjected with an oddly anxious look at Armando.

Armando nodded approvingly. "But you're young and pretty. You must be yearning for some fun." He sighed. "I'm afraid we do not have much social life here. But we must do something to make up for the unpleasantness you have experienced so far. Perhaps a horseback ride? I believe Edith mentioned you enjoyed riding."

"I'm afraid I'm not quite up to that yet," Trish demurred. "I'm sure I'll want a ride later on, but what I'd really like is a tour through the *beneficio*. It sounds fascinating."

"By all means. Any time. Just come to the main office and I'll give you a personally guided tour." Armando sounded pleased with her request, and because he was pleased, Edith practically beamed. He asked about a letter he had mislaid and Edith hurried away to find it for him.

Trish had the uneasy feeling he had sent Edith away on purpose and she was right.

"I understand our neighbor came here to the house to see you while I was absent," he said. He sounded more concerned than angry.

"Yes. I – I don't know why."

"Don't you?" Armando smiled slightly. "I'm sure I do. Marcantonio de la Barca is not one to ignore a lady as young and lovely as you. But be careful of him, Trish. He is not to be trusted. He would have no compunction at all about using you for his own purposes."

"I'm sure I don't know how I could be useful to him," Trish objected. But suddenly, remembering that smoldering glance in her bedroom, she had a very clear notion of just how Marc might find her useful. She felt a flush rising to her skin and concealed it with a sudden, energetic application of suntan lotion.

"Here, you're making a complete mess of that," Armando said disapprovingly. He took the plastic bottle and covered her back thoroughly with the lotion. He stood up as Edith approached with the letter.

"Just remember what I said," he said in a low voice. "I know Marcantonio can be charming and say and do all the things to turn a young lady's head. But do not be deceived by him. This is all just an amusing diversion to him. All he really cares about is himself and possessing this part of the *cafetal*."

Trish was about to tell Armando that he needn't worry, that Marc had so little interest in her that he actually suggested she go home, but Edith interrupted with a comment about

79

the letter. Then Armando was his smiling self again as he departed, waving from the Mercedes as he drove off.

"Did Armando mention Marcantonio's visit to the house?" Edith asked, her eyes following him.

Trish nodded, surprised.

Edith smiled slightly. "I had the feeling that was why he sent me off. Don't be angry if he sounds like a . . . a grumpy father, Trish," she said. "It's just that he is concerned about you and would not want to see you hurt. You have a certain look on your face whenever Marcantonio's name is mentioned."

Trish felt herself flushing again, knowing all too well that just the mention of Marc's name, for some reason she could not explain, sent an unfamiliar fluttery feeling through her. She turned away to hide any more give-away expressions. "When is the seamstress coming?" she asked briskly.

The seamstress arrived a few minutes later with yards and yards of mellow antique-white satin, netting for the veil, seed pearls for decoration, all very expensive and lovely. But Trish looked in dismay at the magazine clipping showing the gown Edith had asked the seamstress to copy for her. It was all wrong for Edith's face and mature figure, far too frilly and fussy. Trish suspected Edith had

80

chosen the style because she thought it looked feminine, and Edith desperately wanted to be soft and feminine for Armando. But Trish knew Edith would only look a little foolish in the frilly style. What Edith needed was something simple but elegant to match her almost queenly face and figure. Trish studied the clipping and finally tactfully pointed out how it could be altered by inserting a single, elegant band of lace in place of the bodice and neckline frills. Edith seemed interested but uncertain, obviously reluctant to abandon what she considered the feminine touches. Edith finally told the seamstress to delay starting the gown until she decided what she wanted to do.

Trish spent the next couple of days completing her recuperation by lazing around the pool. Her skin turned honey tan and the sun enhanced the pale gold of her hair. Edith seldom exposed her skin to the sun and always wore the floppy red hat to protect her face. She enjoyed gardening more than swimming or lounging, and her red hat was a familiar sight bobbing among the shrubs and flowers. There was no sign of Robert Hepler, though Trish occasionally caught glimpses of a white-uniformed woman she assumed was his private nurse.

Sometimes Trish wondered dreamily, as she

gazed up at the picture-perfect clouds drifting overhead, what it would be like to spend a lifetime here like this. Not exactly like this, she reflected. Though it was marvelous to spend a few days doing nothing but sunbathing and swimming and sunbathing again, it was hardly a lifetime occupation. No, what would it be like to be the wife of a *cafetal* owner, helping to look after the workers and villagers as Edith did, competently running a full household of servants, raising a family with the man you loved . . . ?

For no particular reason, at least none she could think of, the image of Marc drifted into her mind. Marc – arrogant, domineering, ruthless, obsessed. But was he always that way? Did his eyes soften when he looked at the lush Ramona de Cordoba? Did the sensuous lips curve with laughter, the harsh grip gentle to a caress? There had been something in that lingering, smoldering glance in her bedroom.

And then he had told her to go home!

That thought broke the momentary spell that had enveloped Trish and she leaped up and dived into the pool, her slim, golden body arcing smoothly into the water. She swam until she was tired and by that time Edith was waiting with samples of wedding invitations to show and discuss with her.

The next morning Trish woke with a decidedly restless feeling. The first thing she did was peer out the window in the direction of Marc's house, a gesture that had become almost automatic with her. Only once had she seen him, his lithe, commanding figure unmistakable even from this distance, but the glimpse had left her more disturbed than satisfied. It was evening and he was dressed for something obviously more important than a stroll to the stables to pat Demonio. Probably a business meeting, she had told herself, though the unsettling vision of Ramona de Cordoba's shapely arms warmly welcoming him kept haunting her. She had watched for a long time but she had not seen him return that evening.

At breakfast Trish asked if Edith would like to take a horseback ride that day, but Edith regretfully said this was the day she held a regular monthly meeting with the village women. Edith drove off immediately after breakfast in the older Chevrolet she used around the plantation, and Trish wandered around restlessly. She washed out a few underthings by hand and took a dip in the pool, but somehow she didn't feel like lying indolently in the sun today. The soreness was all gone from her lungs and throat.

With sudden inspiration she decided this

would be a perfect day to hold Armando to his agreement to give her a tour of the *beneficio*. She had no idea what such a tour might entail, and she dressed in sneakers, comfortable jeans and simple cotton blouse.

She already knew that the buildings she had thought were warehouses on the night Marc brought her home were actually the coffee-processing plant, but the walk was farther than it had seemed that night in the car. The back of her blouse clung damply to her skin by the time she arrived. The area bustled with activity, trucks coming and going, the clack of machinery from inside the building. She made her way toward a trim building that appeared to be an office.

A pretty Costa Rican girl dressed very chicly looked up when Trish stepped inside. Trish hoped this smartly dressed young woman was bilingual and, in English, she inquired about Armando. The girl did not have a chance to reply.

"Señor Albéniz has not honored us with his presence today," a hard masculine voice informed her.

Trish looked up, startled, her breath catching as she saw Marcantonio de la Barca regarding her coldly from the doorway of another room. He was dressed in tan slacks and white shirt, the cuffs turned back to reveal leanly muscled forearms, the collar open to the husky column of his throat. He strode toward the young woman's desk, and handed her a sheaf of papers with crisp instructions about their delivery.

His back was to Trish and his dark hair curled crisply against his tanned neck. Broad shoulders narrowed down to lean hips. He turned sharply and Trish's eyes dropped, hoping he had not caught her scrutinizing him. He did not speak until the secretary left and he and Trish were alone on one side of the room. He inspected her with hostile eyes.

"I would think you could find ample opportunity to meet with Armando at the house without interrupting business hours," he suggested arrogantly.

Trish took a wary step backward, trying not to be intimidated by his domineering presence, but not succeeding. She was suddenly aware of Edith's and Armando's warnings about this man; his hostile eyes and hard mouth seemed to confirm every one of those warnings. But she had never been so aware of the pure masculinity of any man as she was at this moment, a masculinity that seemed to overwhelm her. Unwillingly she felt her body reacting to his powerful maleness, a reaction that left her palms damp and voice uncertain.

"Why are you here?" she finally managed to stammer. "I mean – I didn't realize –"

"Economics dictate that our two *cafetals* cooperate in the operation of the coffee-processing plant, despite our personal conflicts," Marc stated dryly.

"I'll just be going then," Trish stated uneasily. "I'll come back sometime when Armando is here."

She took a step toward the door but unexpectedly a steely grip on her arm stopped her. "I do not think it advisable for you to come here again," he said harshly.

"You don't think it advisable!" Trish gasped, astonishment and anger finally breaking the spell of his masculine dominance over her. "I'll have you know I'm here because Armando very courteously agreed to give me a tour of the *beneficio*. And I certainly do not intend to let you tell me the place is off limits to me!"

For a moment longer his powerful grip encircled her arm and his eyes held hers with suspicion and hostility. Trish momentarily thought about trying to break away, but she remembered what had happened the other time she had tried to resist him. She had no desire to find herself in another wrestling match here on the floor in the full view of half a dozen curious office workers. Somehow she

86

knew Marc would have no hesitation about making just such a humiliating scene if she tried to pull away.

"If you don't mind –" she said icily, her eyes on his lean hand gripping her arm.

Unexpectedly he smiled and released her. "If a tour means so much to you, then by all means allow me to show you around," he offered. His eyes glinted with amusement as she shot a surreptitious glance at the office workers across the room to see if they were watching.

They were not. Perhaps, she thought furiously, because it was not unusual for their employer to be overpowering some strange young woman in their midst.

She rubbed her numbed wrist. "Thank you, no," she snapped. "I'll wait for Armando."

"As you wish."

He shrugged, and his easy acceptance of Trish's rejection of his offer somehow annoyed her. "Armando mentioned some problems here at the *beneficio*," she said suddenly, not admitting even to herself that she interjected the subject to prevent Marc from striding away.

"That is true," he agreed. "The quality of the coffee berries Armando produced this year was not high."

"But he said the harvest was good."

87

"Quantity does not necessarily indicate quality."

Quality, Trish knew instinctively, was a matter of pride with Marc, a basic matter that must not be compromised.

"What do you know about coffee before it reaches your cup?" Marc asked suddenly.

"Not much," Trish admitted.

"Come. I'll show you."

His voice, though no longer triumphantly arrogant, was commanding. His light touch on her elbow guided her through the maze of desks and out a rear door. There a truck was just pulling in with a load of ripe coffee berries. He grabbed a handful and selected one perfect, cranberry-red berry. With a pocket knife he cut into it, his strong hands surprisingly dexterous. He explained as he went, showing her how the outer skin covered a soft pulp, which in turn surrounded a tough inner parchment. Inside that was yet another delicate, silvery-colored skin surrounding each of the twin beans. When that was removed, the two beans lay in the palm of his hand, pale and greenish colored.

"Everything we do here is merely an involved process to get the beans dried and to this state," he explained. "Now I'll show you how it is done."

He guided her through the *beneficio*,

explaining that this was what was known as the wet process because water was used in the processing. The ripe berries were first washed and put through machines to remove the outer pulp. Then they were fermented in large cement vats for twelve to twenty-four hours to aid in removal of the sticky substance surrounding the parchment. Then came more washing followed by drying on large, open, concrete patios. The dried beans were then put through hulling machines to remove the parchment and silver skin. Finally they were graded and bagged.

"I'm impressed," Trish admitted finally, as she ran her fingers through a pile of cleaned, dried beans ready for bagging. She sniffed a handful of the beans. "I didn't realize so much work went into a cup of coffee. But I think I'm disappointed that the *beneficio* doesn't smell the way I expected. Somehow I thought it would smell like the biggest cup of coffee in the world."

Marc laughed, a husky sound without his usual patronizing superiority or taunting mockery, the kind of laugh that made Trish ache to say something that would make him repeat the sound and bring that warm light to his eyes. Edith's and Armando's warnings suddenly seemed unreal and far away.

"That coffee smell you miss comes when

89

the beans are roasted. We don't do that here. In fact most roasting is done within the country importing the beans. I imagine those places have an almost irresistible odor."

Irresistible. The word seem somehow fitting as she looked up into his dark eyes. But even as she looked the warmth seemed to fade from them and a certain wariness took its place.

"I suppose you know by now that I have tried for some time to purchase the Hepler property," he said. "Single management could improve the efficiency of the operation considerably."

As he spoke they moved along the walkway, following the exterior of the main building back to the office. She wondered if he was fishing for information about what Armando and Edith had told her.

"I've heard you were interested," she said, carefully keeping her voice neutral.

"The *cafetal* belongs in my family," he said arrogantly. "It was only through an unfortunate set of circumstances that it passed out of my family's hands."

Trish glanced at him in surprise. "I understood you were the only one of your family remaining. And yet you speak of family as if –"

"My family consists not only of those who

90

came before but those who will come after," he said with a kind of superior conviction. He touched her elbow lightly, guiding her around a lush drape of bougainvillea that threatened to block the walkway. "There will be my sons to carry on."

"From what I've heard, you're rather adept at avoiding the institution of marriage." The tart words slipped out before Trish could stop them.

"When the proper woman comes along, I will marry," he said in the same superior tone.

And what, Trish wondered, did he consider "proper"? The dramatic Ramona de Cordoba perhaps: lush, beautifully groomed, gorgeously dressed, no doubt with the proper aristocratic family background. Trish suddenly felt very dowdy in her jeans and well-worn blouse, her face devoid of makeup except for a touch of lipstick. She realized he was looking at her as if perhaps thinking the same things.

"But one must take care of first things first," he added, his voice hardening.

First things meaning the rejoining of the *cafetal* into one unit, Trish thought slowly. Armando knew what he was talking about; owning both portions of the *cafetal* was Marc's obsession. They were almost back to the office now.

"Thank you for the tour," Trish said, feeling a little awkward now. "You were very helpful."

"Somehow I think that Armando will be less appreciative of my helpfulness," Marc said dryly.

That could be true, Trish thought in dismay, thinking how eagerly Armando had reacted to her interest in the tour of the *beneficio*. She glanced uneasily down the dusty road, suddenly thinking how awkward it would be if he were to drive up just now.

Marc was standing on the steps to the office, a slight smile playing around his sensuous mouth as if perhaps reading her thoughts. It was possible, Trish thought suddenly, that he had given her the tour with the deliberate intent of angering Armando. That certainly seemed the only explanation for the unexpected visit he had made to the house. In spite of his professed interest in "everything about her," he had certainly made no effort to pursue that supposed interest.

"Thanks again for all your time and trouble," Trish said formally. She turned and started up the dusty road.

"Miss Bellingham!"

In spite of her determination to keep moving, the commanding voice stopped her in her tracks. Reluctantly she turned to face him.

"Yes?"

"I'm driving into San José this afternoon. Would you care to accompany me? I have some business to attend to first but we could have dinner afterward."

Trish was so surprised that it was only with effort that she kept her mouth from literally dropping open. She hesitated, her emotions vacillating wildly. She was again aware of Armando's warnings and her own flaming recognition of how Marc might find her "useful." She remembered the cold hostility with which he had greeted her today and his former harsh suggestion that she go away. One part of her wanted to tell him with icy aloofness that she did not care to dine with an arrogant stranger who first treated her with cold hostility and unwarranted suspicion and then expected her to jump at the chance to eat with him, but the other part of her simply rejected all the warnings both from without and within her and shouted yes, yes, yes!

One slim hand played nervously with the bottom button of her plain blouse while she weighed and rationalized the decision already made within her. "I would like the opportunity to look for some special lace for Edith's wedding gown," she said finally.

"Good. We'll leave immediately after lunch," he said briskly. He turned toward the door, dismissing her, then glanced back. "And wear something feminine. I get tired of women in pants all the time."

Trish gasped in indignation, a furious retort rising to her lips, but it was too late. He was already disappearing inside, mocking her with a flashing smile thrown over his shoulder.

She covered the distance back to the house rapidly, her mind running at an even more furious pace than her slim legs. Now she could think of any number of sharp retorts and remarks she should have made, including one that she certainly did not intend to let any man tell her how to dress.

In her room she paced back and forth, telling herself she was not going to go anywhere with a man as insufferable as Marcantonio de la Barca. But even as she was telling herself that, she was riffling through the clothes in her closet, digging out a pair of almost frivolously feminine high-heeled sandals, skimming out of her jeans and blouse and into the shower.

She ate a hurried lunch and couldn't have said five minutes later what she had eaten. Within a quarter hour after lunch she was eyeing her image in the mirror, assuring herself that she had chosen the filmy, scoop-necked dress because it was cooler than a pantsuit and not because of anything Marc had said. In truth she preferred something dressy and feminine for a dinner date, so it would have been foolish to change her personal preferences just to prove to Marc he couldn't boss her around, she rationalized.

She debated about how to handle telling Edith and Armando about her absence, quite certain they would disapprove of any association with Marc. Finally she left a short note for Edith, commenting lightly in it that perhaps she could act as a peacemaker between the two feuding *cafetales*.

She went out to the courtyard to wait for Marc, suddenly realizing he evidently intended to drive to the house to pick her up in spite of Armando's antagonism. Or did Marc intend that she should hike back down to the *beneficio* in her dress and high-heeled sandals? Actually she wouldn't put it past him, she thought wryly. And, a bit ruefully, she suspected she just might do it if she had to.

She sat in the shade under the protective overhang of the wide roof, from where she could see the road. In spite of her good view she got up every few moments to pace past the courtyard gates to make sure she hadn't missed anything. Once she was almost sure she saw the Mercedes and her uneasiness increased. Edith and Armando had made it plain that Marc was, if not an open enemy, at least an adversary. Was she being rude, perhaps even disloyal, in having anything to do with him?

Her thoughts were interrupted as an expensive Italian sports car drove up and braked to a smooth stop in front of the house. Marc stepped out.

"I'm coming!" Trish called, stopping him before he was more than a step away from the car. She saw no point in wasting time and perhaps encountering Armando at the last minute. Hastily she slipped through the gates and ran to meet him, a little breathlessly by the time she slid inside the door he held open for her.

He had changed clothes, smoothly sophisticated now in a well-cut suit and tie and even more intensely masculine. Once seated beside her, he raised a questioning eyebrow at her hasty actions.

"I was afraid . . . I mean, Armando –"

"I can take care of Armando," he said calmly.

Trish tried to minimize his actions, reminding herself he probably knew Armando was away for the day and that there was no danger of encountering him. But somehow she knew Marc meant exactly what he said. He could take care of Armando.

They exchanged some polite comments about the weather and the beautiful countryside, but Marc did not seem particularly inclined to talk. Trish kept thinking about that visit he had made to the house when he harshly suggested she leave, but now that the opportunity was at hand she was somehow reluctant to question him about his unfriendly advice.

They passed a steep side road marked with an unreadable, faded sign, and Trish inquired about it. Marc said the road went to the village where most of the *cafetal* workers lived. Another much plainer sign warned PELIGRO, that the road was dangerous. Trish turned to look back at the mountain looming behind them, a scarf of cloud caught on its tip, and remarked that she had heard his grandfather could remember when steam rose from the mountain. Marc said yes and did not elaborate.

Trish finally gave up on small talk and concentrated on the lush green scenery, trying to ignore Marc's masculine presence that somehow dominated her even in silence. She marveled at vegetation both strange and familiar. Incredibly lovely calla lilies grew wild, seemingly considered almost as weeds as they clambered over pasture fences. There were brilliant poinsettias and hibiscus, hydrangeas, a strange plant with huge leaves that resembled elephant ears, and flowering trees. Giant ferns filled steep ravines. They passed a varied assortment of vehicles on the road, everything from old-fashioned ox-drawn carts to lumbering trucks and makes of cars Trish had never seen before.

Finally, quite abruptly, Marc said, "Tell me about yourself."

Trish was a bit taken aback by the remark, which sounded more like a command than a request. "I've already told you about my relationship with Edith and how I happen to be here," she said coolly. But slowly, encouraged by his questions, she went on to tell him about her parents and her Minnesota childhood with her grandparents, her partial college education, even her vague feeling of drifting rather aimlessly in life.

"Your decision to come to Costa Rica was a rather impulsive one then?" he asked.

"You mean because you didn't know ahead of time that I was coming and you always know everything that is going on?" she returned lightly, remembering his quick knowledge of the fire in her room.

He shrugged. "I was aware that Edith had a half-sister. But you do not resemble each other to any great extent."

They were on the outskirts of San José

98

by now, passing through pleasant residential suburbs with an abundance of flamboyantly flowering trees.

"Armando attended an agricultural college in the States for a time before coming to work for the Heplers," he commented casually. "Could that have been the same college you attended?"

Trish had the sudden, peculiar feeling that this entire conversation, perhaps even the purpose of the dinner invitation, was to lead up to that single question. Did Marc have the mistaken impression that she knew some information about Armando that Marc could use against him? She gave him a sideways glance, but his handsome face was inscrutably expressionless. Trish was suddenly reminded that Armando had said Marc might use her for his own purposes. Perhaps she had been flattering herself to think that those purposes had anything at all to do with her personally even in a temporary, physical sense.

"You asked me once before if I had met Armando in the States and I told you no," she said sharply. Deep down she knew she was more hurt than angry, since it now appeared that Marc's invitation had been prompted by some ulterior motive rather than an honest desire to be with her. "I thought this was supposed to be a dinner date, but if it is a question-and-answer time, perhaps I have some for you!"

He raised a languid eyebrow.

"Why . . . why did you tell me to go away?" she asked, her voice unexpectedly shaky now that the words were out.

"I thought it would be for the best." His voice hardened. "I still think it would be, but somehow I doubt that you're the sort of woman who would take my, or any man's, advice."

"And I'm sure you're the sort of man who prefers an obedient, submissive sort of woman!"

An amused smile curved his lips. "Perhaps." He reached over to brush a strand of hair away from the nape of her neck. "But I also like one with a bit of spirit. And you're right, this is a dinner date." His voice suddenly became brisk. "Our small country has a surprising variety of continental cuisine available. I know an excellent French restaurant that I am sure is the equal of any at which you have dined in the States."

That was undoubtedly true, Trish thought, since she had never dined in a French restaurant in her life. His hand lingered on the bare skin at the nape of her neck and she was oddly conscious of two completely

100

opposite sensations – that his hand was cool to the touch and yet her skin felt on fire beneath the gently moving fingers. The pressure of his hand increased, massaging the muscles from neck to shoulder gently.

"Your muscles are tight as wires," he chided. "Why are you so tense?"

"Just ... just a little nervous. New place and the fire and all," she stammered lamely. But she knew quite well why every muscle and nerve in her body was tense with awareness, and that it had nothing at all to do with the place or the fire but only with the man sitting so coolly, calmly next to her. Why, she thought in sudden frustration, didn't she affect him the way he affected her?

"Well, here we are," he said briskly, removing his hand. "My business won't take more than a few minutes and then we'll find Edith's lace and do a bit of sight-seeing before dinner."

"Fine," Trish agreed, half relieved, half disappointed when his hand left her skin. She peered around. "In fact, that appears to be a fabric shop right over there."

They got out on opposite sides of the sports car and headed in opposite directions. The street was typical of San José, narrow and busy, crowded with both vehicles and people. Trish stopped short, remembering she had never changed any American money into Costa Rican *colones*. Perhaps Marc could change a few dollars for her or tell her where to do it.

She turned and hurried in the direction he had taken, pausing on the corner to search for his tall, commanding figure. There he was, just turning into the doorway of some professional offices.

Trish hurried forward again, her eyes on the door he had entered. There was a discreet sign: HANS SCHWARZ, LICENCIADO.

Trish paused, her mind hesitating first over the name, jarringly German, and then over translation of the other word. Then she had it. *Licenciado* meant lawyer. Marc was going to see an attorney.

Trish couldn't specifically account for her abrupt action. She only knew some sixth sense prompted her to retreat quickly, before Marc turned at the reception desk and spotted her. She remembered Edith's quiet but ominous declaration that Marc had not lessened his determination to own the Hepler *cafetal*.

And she had the uneasy feeling that she had all too willingly been enticed into the camp of the enemy for dinner and that Marc's calculated intentions might well involve using her for his own devious means.

102

Chapter Five

Trish stretched deliciously, the first thing meeting her eye the glorious, deep purple blooms of *guaría morada* that Marc had bought for her from a street vendor the afternoon before – not just one but a full bouquet of the beautiful orchids, Costa Rica's national flower. Then they had toured the National Theater, dined on a heavenly concoction of seafood in a sinfully rich sauce, and washed it down with a heady wine in the intimate setting of the French restaurant Marc had chosen.

Something nibbled at the edge of Trish's mind, something unpleasant, but she refused to let it eat its way into her happiness.

The National Theater, a three-quarter scale reproduction of the Comédie Française in Paris, had been fantastic. Marc had held her hand as they strolled across gleaming parquet floors and lush carpeting, climbed the marble staircase, peered into the luxurious box seats, gazed at the enormous, ornate chandelier. He had steadied her with an arm around her shoulders as they looked up at the delicate murals adorning the ceiling. His darkly handsome face had smiled back at her from the tall mirrors framed in gold curlicues.

His conversation over dinner had been warm and intimate as he talked about his boyhood on the *cafetal*, complimented her on her sparkling eyes, her choice of dress, and the creamy smoothness of her skin. The vision of the lovely Ramona de Cordoba that had occasionally haunted Trish seemed very dim and far away.

And when he brought her home, boldly walking her to the carved doors, he had kissed her. . . .

Trish's heart tripped erratically at the very memory of his mouth against hers and she closed her eyes, bringing back each pulsing moment. Her palms were damp as she raised up on one elbow to peer out the window in the direction of Marc's house, but though she waited hopefully for several minutes, she had no glimpse of him. All she saw was the stallion Demonio staring contemptuously in her direction, as if he could see into her very window. There was something in the proud toss of his head that uneasily reminded Trish of Marc's earlier arrogance.

Trish rested her head on the pillow again, trying to bring back the delicious aura that had enveloped her when she first awakened, but somehow the spell was broken. The unpleasant thoughts she had pushed into the background of her mind refused to be ignored any longer.

Marc had gone to see a lawyer. He had stayed a considerable length of time, long enough for Trish to examine thoroughly every length of lace in the fabric store. He had returned in good spirits, brushing off her attempts to repay him in American dollars when he paid for the lace in *colones*.

There were any number of reasons he could have had for going to see an attorney, Trish reminded herself. He was a powerful, busy man, no doubt with many investments and business matters that required legal attention. But Trish couldn't escape the ominous feeling that his appointment with the lawyer had to do with his obsession to possess the Hepler *cafetal*, that matters were stirring beneath the surface like the invisible mutterings of a long quiescent volcano about to erupt.

And on an even more personally disquieting note was her unhappy feeling that Marc had taken her to dinner for the sole purpose of charming out of her information about Armando, which he seemed to think she possessed.

Trish determinedly brushed those thoughts aside and went looking for Edith after breakfast, wanting to show her the lace and discuss the wedding gown. She could not find

105

Edith, however, and one of the servants finally informed her that the *señorita* was spending the morning with her father.

Trish did not see Edith until just before lunch. Edith tapped on Trish's bedroom door while Trish was dressing after a dip in the pool. Trish opened the door a crack and then widened it to let her in.

"Let me show you the lace I found," Trish said eagerly.

"A little later." Edith seemed preoccupied. "I just wanted to suggest that you not mention anything to Armando at lunch about your trip to San José with Marc. I made excuses for you last night at dinner."

"Yes, of course," Trish agreed. She hesitated. "I suppose I shouldn't have gone, but I wanted to look for the lace."

Edith smiled faintly. "I'm sure Marc can be very charming and persuasive."

Trish felt her fair skin flush slightly. She turned back to the mirror and gave her hair a quick swipe with the brush. "But what if Marc mentions it to Armando?" she asked, eyeing Edith in the mirror.

"We shall have to hope that does not happen," Edith said flatly.

Trish disliked the vaguely underhanded quality all of this gave her impulsive trip with Marc, but there was no point in adding

106

fuel to the fire of Armando's hatred of Marc. Armando undoubtedly would be especially unhappy that she had gone with Marc after he had taken the trouble to warn her about him. Trish considered telling Edith about Marc's visit to the lawyer, but decided against that also. She linked her arm with Edith's as they approached the dining room together and was gaily inquiring horseback riding when Armando rose to greet them.

"Ah, Trish, you must be feeling better today," he said.

Trish looked at him blankly for a moment, then remembered Edith's excuses. "Yes, I'm fine now. I was just asking Edith about taking a horseback ride."

They settled around the table and a servant brought salads and an unusual and surprisingly delicious cream of avocado soup. Edith barely ate, however. She looked distinctly uneasy and kept giving Trish nervous little glances, as if afraid Trish might forget and make some mention of her trip with Marc. Trish determinedly kept the conversation headed in another direction, asking about places to ride.

"There's a good trail to the village that is shorter than the road," Armando suggested. "Or, if you're feeling ambitious, you might enjoy the ride up Monte Decepción."

"You mean there's a trail all the way to the top of the mountain?" Trish asked with interest. "Oh, I'd love that. What's up there?"

"The view isn't as magnificent as that from Costa Rica's most famous volcano, Irazu," Edith said. "From there you can sometimes see the Pacific Ocean in one direction and the Atlantic in the other."

"But the ride up Decepción is certainly worthwhile also," Armando interjected.

"Would you ride with me?" Trish asked, turning to Edith.

"Of course, I'd love to. I haven't been up there in over a year." Edith smiled, her tension obviously relaxing as she realized there was not going to be an unpleasant scene. "And we really should keep an eye on the old mountain, I suppose."

"Good! Let's go this afternoon then!" Trish said.

Armando laughed. "I'm afraid the mountain is deceptive in more ways than one. The summit is farther up than you might think. It takes all day to ride up and back."

"Tomorrow then?" Trish questioned Edith eagerly.

Edith tilted her head thoughtfully. "Certainly. Why not? We'll have the cook pack a lunch for us, though I haven't ridden for so long that I probably won't be able to

108

walk for a week afterward!"

"Me, too," Trish agreed. She went on to relate a tale of a childhood riding experience when she thought she would surely be bowlegged for life, and soon they were all laughing together. Armando seemed to have recovered completely from his earlier depression or anger about the coffee-quality problems at the processing plant.

That afternoon, while Edith spent more time with her father, Trish located the stables and made friends with the horses. The stables were not as impressive as Marc's breeding establishment, or the quality of the animals as high. A gleaming bay gelding stood out among the other horses, however, and Trish found his friendly manner preferable to Demonio's high-headed contempt.

Afterward Trish inquired of one of the servants about the trail up the mountain and hiked around a couple of its zigzagging curves. The trail appeared a bit overgrown from lack of use but navigable enough. Most of the conversation at dinner that evening centered around Edith's and Trish's plans for the next day. Trish was eagerly looking forward to the ride and hoped it might be an opportunity to develop a closer relationship with Edith. In spite of the length of time Trish had already been at the *cafetal*, she somehow felt she was not really getting to know her half-sister as well as she would like.

That opportunity was not going to come this day, however, Trish realized in disappointment the next morning when she read a hurriedly written note a servant handed her at breakfast. Armando had received word late the previous night that a cousin of his had been involved in a serious auto accident and he and Edith were on their way to see him immediately. They did not want to ruin Trish's riding plans, however, and Edith had ordered a saddled horse brought to the house immediately after breakfast.

Trish was prepared to wait for another day, but then she glanced out the window and saw the trim bay gelding already saddled and waiting for her. The cook brought out a neatly packed lunch, and she decided to go ahead with her plans. She breakfasted quickly, eager to be on her way.

Once outside, she paused. It would be a long day, riding in bright sun most of the time. She had better wear something to protect her fair skin from sunburn. She went back inside and dabbed on suntan lotion. Hurrying back through the courtyard, she impulsively picked up the floppy, bright red hat Edith frequently wore. The wide brim would shade her eyes as well as protect her face, and she knew Edith wouldn't mind if she borrowed it.

Trish mounted the alert gelding and as they started up the trail he seemed as interested and eager as she was. It was a glorious morning, bright, yet not uncomfortably warm. The trail first passed through an area of wild shrubbery, but then followed along the edge of the cultivated area.

The coffee trees were laid out in a neat, uniform pattern. They were smaller than Trish had expected, not much more than bushes actually. They appeared to have been pruned to keep them to a standard height. Trish reined the gelding to a halt by one of them and reached out to touch a glossy leaf, dark green on the upper side, a lighter shade on the lower. This tree had already been stripped of its ripe coffee berries, but workers were still picking in the distance. As she watched, a loaded truck lumbered off toward the *beneficio*, and Trish marveled that each coffee berry in that big load had been individually picked by a human hand.

She rode on then, the panorama of the *cafetales* spreading out below as she gained height on the mountain. Larger trees were scattered among the smaller coffee trees, evidently to offer shade during part of the day. They looked benevolently protective, like

111

a mother hen stretching her wings over her little chicks.

The voices of the workers carried a long distance in the clear mountain air, but eventually Trish climbed beyond hearing distance. The gelding worked up a light sweat and Trish rested him frequently. From here she could see both houses, with the *beneficio* perched on what appeared to be an approximate dividing line between the properties. A couple of vehicles moved near the buildings, but from here it was impossible to identify them.

Was Marc in his office today? Did he ever think about the afternoon and dinner they had shared together? If he did, his viewpoint was probably considerably different from hers, Trish thought ruefully. To him it had probably been a waste of time, since she had been unable, or, from his viewpoint, perhaps unwilling, to tell him anything incriminating about Armando. And yet, when he kissed her, he had seemed as passionately involved in the moment as she had been.

She shivered lightly. The sunshine was still incredibly bright, but at this altitude the air had chilled considerably. The perspiration under the band of the floppy red hat had dried, yet Trish knew that shiver had more to do with her memory of Marc's kiss than the mountain temperature. She looked around, hungrily eyeing the lunch tied to the back of the saddle, but she decided to wait until she reached the summit to eat.

She touched the horse with her heels. She had not brought riding boots to Costa Rica and she was wearing only soft-soled canvas shoes, but the gelding responded willingly to the light touch. Here the trail departed from its zigzag course and circled around to the far side of the mountain. A new panorama stretched before Trish's eyes. She caught her breath at the sight of green mountains fading to blue in the distance, the familiar wisps of clouds caught on the peaks. She glanced upward and in surprise saw that a similar cloud was now caught on Monte Decepción itself. Up close, the cloud looked considerably less wispy and ethereal and more like a chilling fogbank.

She hesitated, undecided, as she looked at the grim uninviting scene rising above her. She had kept her eyes mostly on what lay below, but now she noted that the vegetation along the trail had thinned to stunted shrubs. Above her the slopes were almost barren, the fog swirling and shifting in wraithlike shapes. Once she thought she saw something move, but then she realized it was only a trick of the fog, the mists curling around an angular rock

113

perched precariously against the slope.

Perhaps she should turn back, she thought uneasily. It looked as if it wouldn't take much to start the loose jumble of volcanic rock along the trail hurtling off in a wild avalanche. If she lost her way or the horse accidentally stepped off the trail . . .

That was ridiculous, she told herself firmly. The trail was plain enough under the horse's feet, even though visibility was now down to only a few feet ahead of her. Edith and Armando would have warned her if there was any danger coming up here. It would be a shame to turn around now when the goal of the summit was so close. Obviously her decision to eat lunch at the summit was impractical, but she would ride on up to the top, just to be able to say she had been there, and then ride back down to the sunshine for lunch.

That decision made, she urged the gelding on. He seemed a little less eager now, almost apprehensive, and his nostrils flared slightly. His shod feet crunched against the fine volcanic rock. There was no echo or other sound and yet Trish found herself glancing backward frequently, her ears listening nervously for some sound just out of hearing range. The trailing, shifting fog gave a peculiar sense of motion to the

114

big rocks as they disappeared and reappeared in the white mist, a feeling of lurking shapes seen just out of the corner of her eye. Once she pulled the horse up sharply, half expecting to hear muffled hoofbeats or footsteps continue behind her, but there was nothing but the sound of the gelding's hard breathing.

She rode through an area of jagged, jumbled boulders, wondering apprehensively if just the thud of the horse's hooves could send them into thundering motion. But she passed through without a rock moving so much as a fraction of an inch. They had probably been precariously perched just that way for years, maybe centuries, she told herself, trying to laugh at her imaginings.

The trail ended abruptly, without warning, and Trish caught her breath as she reined the gelding up sharply.

"Easy, boy," she soothed, not wanting to convey her nervousness to him. She leaned forward, peering over his shoulder into the seemingly bottomless abyss only inches ahead of him.

It probably wasn't as deep as it appeared to be, she told herself shakily. She couldn't actually see more than a few feet into the crater because of the fog. Perhaps the bottom was only a few feet away from her.

But somehow she knew it wasn't.

115

"Hello, down there!" she called out, feeling foolish and yet needing the reassuring sound of a voice, even if it was only her own.

There was no echo, no answer. The mist-filled pit seemed to swallow her voice whole. She looked a moment longer at the barren slope of the crater angling steeply away from her and abruptly reined the horse around. There was no view here, nothing to see, and she was anxious to get away from this chilling spot that gave her the sinking feeling of being on the edge of the world with some unknown hell waiting far below.

The noise was so sharp, so unexpected, that for a moment it didn't really register on Trish. She almost thought she had imagined it. Then it came again . . . and again. Gunshots. Gunshots so sharp and close, they split the air around her.

The quiet horse went rigid beneath her. He flung his head into the air and the reins drooped slackly as his eyes rolled backward at Trish, the edges white with terror.

"Easy, boy," Trish soothed, dismayed at his strange reaction. She reached down to pat his trembling shoulder, but instinctively she knew he was beyond control of her voice or hands, that some internal terror shut out everything else.

She shifted her weight in the saddle,

preparing to ease to the ground and try to calm him from there. She had ridden horses that acted up playfully or shied when startled, but never one that reacted like this, with petrified terror. She could actually feel the beat of his powerful heart throbbing through his trembling body.

Another gunshot cracked. The frozen muscles exploded. Trish had one foot out of the stirrup when the horse reared violently. She felt herself flung backward into nothingness, into that bottomless abyss. The sound of her own voice shrieked around her, and then she hit, falling, rolling . . .

She came to slowly, her mind crawling up from some mist-shrouded emptiness. There was a sound, a strange, muffled roaring in her ears. She lay there, trying to identify it, trying to bring her eyes to focus on something, but there was only the swirling, changing mist, the smell of damp and cold. Her mind seemed as lacking in solidity as the wisps of white mist curling around her. She lay motionless, trying to orient herself, half expecting that this was all some nightmare that would fade as she wakened to find herself in bed.

But it was no nightmare. At least not an imaginary one.

Her eyes focused now. The swirling mist

117

blotted out the crater depths below her and the rim above her, but she knew she was somewhere between them on the steep, barren slope. There were no sounds. The silence was so complete that it was the internal workings of her own body that roared in her ears.

Something was poking her painfully in the back and she moved tentatively. Then she realized she had better not complain because the scraggly shrub was all that had stopped her tumbling roll to the bottom. Tentatively she moved again. She was sore all over, her clothing ripped and torn, but miraculously nothing seemed broken.

Carefully she edged herself into a lengthwise position against the steep slope, one foot braced against the shrub as she worked her way upward, trying to keep her mind away from what would happen if she slipped. Her fingers clawed uselessly at the loose volcanic rock at first, but finally she found another clump of hardy vegetation to which to cling.

She had no idea how far she was from the top, but gradually her eyes made out the line of jagged rocks that marked the rim. She couldn't go straight up the slope, and had to work back and forth, following the growth of stunted shrubs. But finally, her

118

fingernails broken to the quick, she crawled over the edge and rested, panting, her heart thundering with exertion.

The horse was nowhere in sight, but something lay on the ground where he had been. Trish staggered to it. The hat. The floppy red hat, the brim shredded now by the horse's flailing hooves.

She leaned against one of the rocks, resting, holding her aching side. What had happened to the horse? It wasn't surprising that the gunshots had frightened him, but he had been more than startled. He had gone crazy with terror. And why, she wondered, baffled for a moment, would anyone be hunting and shooting up here?

Then it hit her at once and she started shaking uncontrollably. Gunshots! There was no game to hunt up here. The hunter had come in search of only one quarry – Trish herself!

Were the shots meant to kill her outright or send the horse into a frenzy of terror? What did it matter? Someone had tried to kill her!

Trish bit her lip, willing down the rising hysteria, and tried to think logically. Edith had spent all day yesterday with her father. Was he getting worse, harder to control? He could have known Trish would be riding up

119

here today. Edith might even have told him of their plans, never dreaming he would try to take revenge in this way.

But he was old and ill, Trish reminded herself, momentarily doubtful. He had the full-time care of a nurse. Surely he couldn't have climbed all the way up here and hidden in wait for her ... could he? And yet she knew he wasn't bedridden, knew he got away from the nurse occasionally. She knew, too, how powerfully, how convulsively, his hands had worked in hatred when he saw her. Perhaps this hatred had been further inflamed because she had escaped the first fiery death he'd planned for her. The phrase *the strength of a madman* stabbed into her mind and stayed there. Sometimes madness brought its own strength and made almost superhuman feats possible.

Suddenly Trish jumped to her feet, ignoring the pain of quick movement. He might still be around, lurking in the mist to finish the job he had started.

Then she calmed, though her breath still came in jerks as she glanced around. He was gone. Some inner instinct told her that.

She rested a few minutes longer, then tossed the mangled hat aside and started walking, clutching her tattered blouse around her. When the horse ran into the stable riderless, someone would surely come looking for her, but she had no desire to wait here unprotected on the summit until that time.

The trail led downhill all the way. Trish could, at least, be grateful for that much. She knew she could never have made it if she'd had to climb uphill. The thin soles of her canvas shoes were no match for the volcanic cinders of the trail, and soon it seemed she could feel each rock on her tender feet. But she doggedly struggled on, pausing to rest frequently, her eyes searching hopefully for help from below.

On one of those pauses she looked down and saw something she had missed on the way up. She stared at the area curiously in spite of her weariness and the pain in her feet. It was a peculiar area, like a liquid, blistered hell turned solid, or a tangle of monstrous prehistoric snakes frozen motionless, with here and there some hellish monster rising out of their midst. This must be the area of volcanic tubes and tunnels that Edith had once mentioned. Trish shivered and turned back to the trail. It was not a place she would care to explore.

She struggled on, concentrating on placing one foot in front of the other. She couldn't understand why no one came looking for her. Surely the horse, even terror-stricken as he was, would head for home. And surely someone would notice he had returned without a rider.

And yet no one came. She could see the houses and *beneficio* below. There was no sign of unusual activity, no frantic movement to indicate anyone was worried or looking for her. All was calm and normal.

When she finally reached the cultivated area of coffee trees, she looked around hopefully for a truck, anyone to give her aid. She had not had anything to eat or drink since breakfast. Her mouth felt thick and cottony, her legs weak. But the pickers had moved on to some other area. No one was in sight.

Damn Marc, she thought, suddenly angry. Why wasn't he looking out his office window? Why didn't he come for her? Somehow the fact that she knew her thoughts and anger were totally illogical did nothing to soothe her temper. He should be here to help her, he should know!

She stumbled on, blinking as she approached the house from the side, hardly able to believe she had actually made it. Then she saw what she needed most – water! Water dripping from a faucet at the corner of the house.

She turned the faucet on full blast, cupping

her hands to drink from them, sloshing water over her sun-burned face and dirt-streaked skin. No luxurious bubble bath, no streaming shower, had ever felt more glorious!

She was running damp hands through tangled blond hair when she saw a pickup truck roaring up the road from the *beneficio*, a cloud of dust in its wake. She caught a glimpse of Marc's set, angry face. She stepped back, trying to conceal herself against the shrubbery, suddenly conscious of her torn blouse and ragged appearance. Though she had earlier illogically raged at Marc for not knowing she needed help, suddenly she did not want him to see her in this bedraggled condition, especially not if he was angry about something. She felt in no condition to cope with him in that mood.

She heard the sharp slam of the pickup door and a moment later Marc's angry voice at the house door.

"Where is Armando? I want to see him!" he stormed. "What the hell did he do to that horse?"

The horse! Marc must mean the gelding that had come in without her. But what did he know about the horse? And why was he blaming Armando? Trish couldn't make out the servant's murmured reply, but evidently it did not assuage Marc's anger. Then Trish heard him exclaim her own name.

"Miss Bellingham! Then where the hell is she?"

Trish stepped forward, suddenly angry with his arrogant attitude, intending to tell him with cool aloofness that she was right here, thank you. But all she got out was his name and then her weakened legs wilted beneath her.

"My God, Trish, what happened to you?"

He didn't wait for an answer. He scooped her up in strong arms and she felt herself carried limply to the courtyard gates. She leaned her head against his strong chest without protest and closed her eyes, feeling somehow safe and secure in his arms. She was aware of a vague feeling of regret when he stretched her out on a lounge chair near the pool and released her.

His strong but gentle hands searched for her pulse, and then she felt them moving over her lightly as he inspected her scratches and bruises. The touch felt somehow soothing, comforting to know she was in competent hands. His fingers massaged her temples and in spite of her weariness, her heart beat faster in reaction to his touch. Her eyes drifted open. He was leaning over her, his dark eyes intent, a frown of concentration on his handsome face. But his slightly brooding expression was hardly what Trish had hoped to see.

"It wasn't Armando's fault," she said faintly. "I was riding the horse."

"What happened?" he asked tersely.

"I don't know. He seemed such a quiet, well-mannered horse. But when I got to the top of the mountain, there was a noise and it was all foggy and the horse went wild. He reared and threw me." Trish tugged the scraps of her blouse together, suddenly aware of her exposed bra beneath.

Marc didn't seem to notice. "What kind of noise?"

"I think ... no, I'm sure. It was a gun. Several gunshots."

His hand still on her wrist was almost painfully tight. "You're sure?"

Trish's strength was returning. "I didn't see the gun if that's what you mean," she said, a little annoyed at his doubt. "But I've heard a gunshot before and it certainly sounded familiar."

"You were alone?" He didn't seem to notice the tartness in her voice either.

"Edith planned to go with me, but at the last minute a cousin of Armando's was hurt in a car accident and they went to see him."

Almost as Trish spoke, the Mercedes pulled up in front of the house and stopped. Armando, evidently recognizing Marc's pickup, scowled darkly as he got out. He stalked toward the main entrance to the house, saw the open courtyard gates, and pivoted toward them. Edith was a few paces behind him.

"What is going on here?" Armando demanded angrily as he stepped through the iron gates. His eyes widened when he saw Trish.

Edith looked pale, almost ill. The accident must have been a bad one, Trish thought, her own painful scratches forgotten for the moment.

"Trish has been hurt," Marc said without preliminaries. He looked around, saw a towel hanging on a nearby chair, and flung it at her. She draped it over her torn blouse. Marc turned back to Armando. "What do you mean, sending her up there on that damn fool horse?"

Armando looked at him with an icy cold expression punctuated by hot hatred in his eyes. "I would prefer to hear what Trish has to say."

"First you're going to hear what I have to say," Marc said grimly. "You know that horse goes insane when he hears gunshots –"

"Gunshots!" Armando exclaimed. "I know nothing of the kind! What is this?"

126

Quickly Trish explained everything again, keeping a restraining hand on Marc's arm as he knelt beside her.

"I see," Armando said finally. He looked at Marc. "And what has all this to do with you, *señor?*"

"That horse came galloping into my yard about mid-afternoon. He was lathered with foam from running, his legs all cut up by rocks, the saddle half torn off. My caretaker had no idea where he had come from or what had happened." Marc's eyes, grim as his voice, never left Armando's face. "I was away at the time but the caretaker came to the office after I returned and got me. I recognized the horse immediately. He was born and raised in my stables."

"I did not know that," Armando said stiffly.

Trish had a good idea Armando would never have bought the horse if he had known Marc had owned it first.

"I sold the horse to a man who took some fool hunting on him before the horse had any experience around guns. The tourist used the horse's neck to steady his rifle when he shot. The gun kicked back, and the horse has had an insane reaction to gunshots ever since."

"I knew nothing of this," Armando said coldly. "I am not a hunter and I did not inquire about the horse's performance around

127

guns when I purchased him a few weeks ago."

"Your ignorance came damn near getting Trish killed!" Marc said angrily.

"Please, you must not blame Armando," Edith said faintly. "I was the one who ordered the horse saddled for Trish. I had no idea he might be dangerous."

Armando, heels together, dipped his head slightly to Marc. "I thank you for your observations and your assistance. I shall post signs or guards, if necessary, to see that we do not have careless hunters trespassing on the property in the future. We will take care of Trish now and see that she receives proper medical attention."

"Oh, I'm all right. Just a few scratches and bruises," Trish said hastily. "There was one other casualty though. I was wearing Edith's red hat and it was trampled and torn to pieces."

Edith waved that small matter away with a gesture of dismissal.

At least all this explained why no one had come looking for her, Trish thought, since the horse had run to the home where he had been raised rather than the Hepler stables. Armando naturally assumed the shots had been fired by careless hunters, and here in the security and safety of the courtyard that did seem a logical explanation. Her imagination must have been running away with her up there on the mountain, Trish thought shakily.

Trish glanced over at Edith again. She had slumped into a chair and her usually composed face looked ashen, tight with the effort to control her emotions. Marc was also watching Edith, an odd expression on his face.

"Was Armando's cousin badly hurt?" Trish asked sympathetically.

Edith just sat there, unmoving, and it was Armando who answered aloud.

"We were misinformed about the seriousness of the accident. My cousin is fine, merely a few cuts and bruises."

Trish looked at Edith again, puzzled. If that was the case, why was Edith so upset?

Then, in a rush, the reason dawned on Trish. Edith knew! Marc and Armando were arguing about the horse and its wild reaction to a hunter's gunshot, but Edith suspected who had really fired those shots. And it was no careless hunter. It was Edith's own father!

Another chilling thought suddenly occurred to Trish. Robert Hepler surely could not have known about the gelding's peculiar terror of the sound of gunshot. He had fired those shots with more deliberate intent. To kill.

Trish did not doubt but that he would try again.

Chapter Six

A long stunned period of silence seemed to surround Trish as chilling thoughts about Edith's father raced through her mind. Evidently she was the only one who felt that strange pause in time. No one else appeared to notice anything.

Edith was standing now, murmuring thanks to Marc. Armando, his arms folded, stood with his feet belligerently spread, waiting for Marc to leave. Marc was taking his own good time about doing that, Trish noted, as he casually talked to Edith about a coming fiesta in the nearby village.

Trish thought he had forgotten her, but unexpectedly he turned and looked squarely at her. "Will I see you at the fiesta?"

Trish felt flustered with Armando staring daggers of disapproval at her and Edith eyeing her nervously. "I ... I don't know," Trish stammered. "I suppose it depends on Edith and Armando's plans –"

"Of course," he said curtly. His earlier

130

concern and shock over her injuries seemed to have changed to a cold indifference now. He gave Trish a final calculating glance that seemed to measure her and somehow find her lacking. Then he turned on his heels and strode out the iron gates without looking back.

Armando muttered an oath under his breath. Edith put a placating hand on his arm. She still looked unnaturally pale and troubled. She said something in a low voice that Trish could not make out, and then they both turned to Trish.

Armando forced a smile. "I am sorry. Our neighbor . . . what is the expression . . . rubs me the wrong way."

"We should get Trish to a doctor immediately," Edith said.

"I think a long, hot bath to soak away the soreness and then some antiseptic and Band-Aids will be all I need," Trish said. No further mention was made of the horse or gunshots.

Trish struggled to her feet, surprised to find how her sore muscles had stiffened as she lay in the lounge chair. Edith helped her to the bedroom and ran bath water. A little later, after Trish had bathed, Edith brought a dinner tray with medications and bandages. She didn't leave immediately and Trish had the impression she wanted to talk but didn't know how to get started.

"I'm glad to hear Armando's cousin wasn't badly injured," Trish offered for openers as she buttered a slice of home-baked bread.

Edith nodded almost absentmindedly. Finally she said ruefully, "You must think only terrible things happen here. First the fire and now this awful accident."

So that was the way it was going to be, Trish thought slowly as she took a sip of the hot, bracing coffee. The gunshots were going to be treated as an accident and no mention ever made of Edith's father.

When Trish didn't answer, Edith added, "You're not thinking about leaving, are you?"

Again her voice held an anxious note, the obvious fear that Trish would desert her. As their mother had long ago deserted her? Trish wondered. She looked at Edith compassionately, wondering what pain, loneliness, and fear of rejection lay hidden beneath her composed exterior.

"Of course I'm not leaving. My grandmother always said I was accident prone," Trish finally said lightly. "When I was small I fell out of bed so many times they finally put up a railing."

Edith smiled, obviously relaxing. "You'll enjoy the fiesta," she said eagerly. "There's

132

a marvelous parade and games, music, and dancing. Everyone looks forward to it all year."

Trish lifted an eyebrow. "What about Marc? Will Armando go if Marc is going to be there?"

"Everyone goes," Edith assured her. "All the owners of the surrounding *fincas* and *cafetales* will be there, plus all the villagers and workers, of course. Everything else stops while the fiesta is on. I know you will enjoy it. You must think about the fiesta and forget about these . . . unfortunate accidents."

Trish nodded slowly. She didn't want to bring up the subject of Edith's father and yet she didn't think she could totally ignore him either, after what had happened.

"How is your father these days?" she finally asked tentatively.

Edith looked down at her hands, her fingers playing with the engagement ring on her left hand. "I hate the thought, but the time may come when I must take him somewhere else. Someplace where he can receive more intensive treatment for his . . . problems."

Obviously Edith was reluctant to talk about her father. "Would you mind if I asked you to postpone your morning swim until later in the day tomorrow?" she finally asked, as if also reluctant to make the request. "I stopped in

133

to see Father for a few minutes while you were taking your bath and he said he would like to take a swim in the morning. His legs are bothering him."

Trish quickly assured Edith that she would keep out of sight until after Mr. Hepler's swim, but another dismaying thought suddenly occurred to her. Was there some special reason that his legs were bothering him? Such as a strenuous hike up the mountain and back?

"It's nice that your father is still able to enjoy swimming," Trish said uneasily. "I never see him outside."

Edith pressed her lips together, as if suddenly realizing that her request had perhaps revealed too much. "Let me know if you need more antiseptic or bandages," she said, quickly changing the subject.

Trish finished her dinner slowly, thoughtfully, her feelings mixed. She was not sure Edith was doing the right thing in choosing to ignore the possibility of her father's involvement in today's accident, but she couldn't help but feel a certain admiration for Edith's unswerving loyalty. After dinner Trish faced the unpleasant task of dabbing antiseptic on her various cuts and scratches. Though the task was painful, she had only to think what injuries she might have sustained

134

to be grateful for these minor wounds.

The next morning a servant brought breakfast to Trish's bedroom, evidently having been previously instructed by Edith to do so. Trish washed out a few underthings by hand in the bathroom and manicured what remained of her broken fingernails.

Then curiosity got the better of her. Carefully she slipped out of her room and around the hallway corner to the one place she knew she could observe the swimming pool while remaining hidden.

The door to her former room was unlocked and Trish slipped inside quietly. The window had been repaired. The odor of smoke was gone, replaced now by the smell of fresh paint. Even the singed curtains and drapes had been replaced.

Trish cautiously lifted a corner of the filmy curtain to get a better view, careful to make no quick movement that might attract attention from outside.

Edith, in a rather heavy, one-piece blue bathing suit, was standing in the shallow end of the water. The middle-aged nurse was kneeling by the edge of the pool. Edith's father, only part of his head visible to Trish, was evidently hanging on to the side of the pool and kicking slowly to exercise his legs. After several minutes he rested, still sitting

135

in the water, and then slowly swam two laps around the pool with Edith following barefoot on the walkway.

Finally, using the tubular railing for assistance, he climbed out of the pool. The nurse handed him a towel and he walked partway around the pool to take a lounge chair only a few feet from the window where Trish watched.

Seen like this, in broad daylight, he was hardly the fearsome monster of the midnight hallway encounter. His tall figure was almost painfully thin, the arms looking disproportionately long and the hands unusually large because of their gaunt boniness. Ill health had taken the flesh from his face, but his deep-set eyes looked more sad than menacing. He did have a rather disconcerting habit of opening and closing his hands, but it was hardly a threatening gesture as Trish had taken it to be in the hallway that night. He reached down to massage the calf of his thin leg and Trish let the curtain fall back into place, doubt assailing her. It was possible, she supposed, that his bad legs today were a result of a strenuous trip up the mountain yesterday. And yet, looking at those wasted muscles, she found that difficult to believe.

She watched a minute more, thinking of the way he had whispered her mother's name that night and the panic he had aroused in her. But all she could feel for him now was pity. Obviously once a fine specimen of a man, he was now stooped and weakened by illness.

Bewildered, Trish let herself out of the room and went back to stare absently out the window of her own room. If Robert Hepler, inflamed by hatred for the woman who had deserted him for another man, had not climbed the mountain to fire those shots at her, who had? She had no other enemies here, nor, she hoped fervantly, enemies anywhere who would resort to murder to get rid of her.

And yet the shots had been fired.

She lay on the bed, her chin resting on her doubled fists, her eyes seeing but not really noticing the horses grazing peacefully in Marc's pasture. The shots had been fired at close range, she was sure of that, close enough for even a mediocre marksman to hit his target . . . her . . . at least once. Since she had not been hit, the aim must have been to frighten the horse into a violent frenzy and let the poor, terrorized animal do the dirty work so that her death would look like an accident. That meant the assailant had to be someone who was aware of that peculiar characteristic about the horse.

Marc knew.

The thought leapt unbidden into Trish's

137

mind. Alarmed and dismayed, she tried to push it back. Marc had no reason to harm her. The very idea was ridiculous.

And yet ... he had had the opportunity to fire the shots. He had admitted he was not in his office when the lathered horse galloped in, that the caretaker had notified him later when he returned. Returned from where? A hurried climb on the mountain? Marc's superb physical condition would have enabled him to make the trip up and down the mountain easily, no doubt about that.

But he had no way of knowing about her plans, she argued with herself.

No, that was not true, she realized with a sinking feeling. Marc had already proved, through his knowledge of the fire in her room, that he knew what was going on in the Hepler household. Through the servants he could easily have kept track of her plans and movements.

No! It simply could not be! Marc had been completely surprised and shocked by her injuries and what had happened on the mountain. Or was a consummate acting skill just another of his many and varied talents? Perhaps his real shock and surprise had been in finding her alive and back at the house after he had left her for dead in the fog-filled mountain crater. He couldn't climb down

138

to check and make certain she was dead, of course. That would have left tracks and raised doubt about the accidental nature of her death. And there had been that odd, brooding look on his face when she opened her eyes in the courtyard.

Trish sat up abruptly. Now her imagination was really running away with her! She was getting paranoid over what were probably just a couple of unfortunate if oddly coincidental accidents. There was nothing at all to link Marc with the fire and certainly no reason for him to harm her.

Peculiar accidents were not all that foreign to her anyway, she reminded herself firmly. Her grandmother had once remarked that Trish was the only person she knew who managed to catch her hair in the electric mixer and practically scalp herself. And her high school chemistry teacher had lived in mortal fear of Trish's lab experiments.

Trish laughed at herself shakily, reminding herself again that Marc had absolutely no reason to harm her, much less murder her. She might not be his idea of the perfect dinner date, since she certainly lacked Ramona de Cordoba's extravagant beauty and sophistication, but that was hardly a crime worthy of death, even to the arrogant, aristocratic Marcantonio de la Barca.

Trish jumped up and busied herself straightening the room. It was a beautiful day and she was not going to lie around and dwell on wild suspicions. The thought did occur to her that sound carried a long distance on the mountain. Perhaps the gunshots were nowhere nearly as close as she had imagined and their effect on the horse really just an unfortunate accident.

Edith lunched with her father and came around later to thank Trish rather awkwardly for her cooperation concerning the pool. The seamstress came that afternoon. Trish brought out the lace she had chosen and made a quick sketch of how the pattern could be altered to give an elegant rather than frilly effect. Edith seemed truly grateful, remarking in embarrassment that she had no sense of style at all. Trish's heart went out to her, thinking how difficult it must have been growing up in a motherless household. Later they discussed food and drink for the wedding reception. Edith even blushingly asked Trish's opinion of honeymoon locations.

It was a pleasant afternoon and the next few days passed equally pleasantly. Trish worked the soreness out of her muscles by exercising in the pool, and the cuts and scratches were healing nicely. There was a growing excitement in the air as the fiesta approached.

Trish could sense it among the servants and she found herself looking forward to it with rising anticipation.

The fiesta was just something new and different, she assured herself. The chance that she might see Marc again had nothing to do with her anticipation. She had to admit she was rather disappointed that he had made no effort to see or contact her again since the day of her disaster on the mountain. A few casual inquiries to Edith – though Trish suspected Edith knew the inquiries were not all that casual – brought the information that Marc was probably very involved in the fiesta plans. He usually furnished meat for the *asado* and prizes for the various contests and games. Armando, Edith added with pride, was providing a magnificent fireworks display this year and would be setting it off himself.

On the opening day of the three-day fiesta Edith and Trish took the older car Edith used around the plantation and drove to the village immediately after breakfast to be sure of arriving in time for the parade. Armando had to drive into San José to pick up the last of the fireworks for the evening display. Trish saw many groups of people making their way up the steep, crooked road to the village, but there was no sign of Marc.

Edith parked the car in a cleared area

141

just before reaching the village, remarking laughingly that later on the one main street was usually so thronged with people that it was impossible to drive through. They walked from the car. The village was larger than Trish had realized. The frame houses were modest but neat and comfortable looking, with bright flowers in tin-can pots decorating the steps and porches. Chickens, dogs, and children wandered freely, and there was the occasional bleat of a goat or squeal of a pig. In the distance near the church, Trish could see the parade forming.

A small reviewing stand of board seats had been erected for important people. Edith and Trish found places about halfway up, Trish sitting on the outside edge. Edith introduced Trish to the wives of several other plantation-farm-owners in the surrounding area. There was animated discussion about the coming wedding that brought the flattering glow of pleasure and excitement to Edith's face and made her plain features handsome. Her love for Armando was written all over her whenever his name was mentioned. And how marvelous that that love was returned, Trish thought, feeling momentarily depressed, though she couldn't explain why.

The parade was late getting started, which no one seemed to find surprising. It finally began solemnly with at least ten men carrying a platform on which rested in colorful splendor an effigy of the patron saint of the village. Edith explained that once a year it was carried to the spring that supplied water for all the village and then carried back at the end of the fiesta. This was, in fact, what the fiesta was all about.

But once the platform was safely deposited, the solemnity ended and an exuberant almost reckless air took over. A flamboyant marimba band set the tone. A clown pranced along the sidelines, amusing the excited children. There was a flower-decorated float of pretty girls. Bells jangled, dogs barked, and roosters crowed. Then came the oxcarts, this a bit more serious because they were being judged and a large prize was at stake. The oxcarts were decorated with incredibly intricate paintings, the solid wooden wheels a sunburst blaze of colors, the car sides a swirl of flowers, vines, and geometric designs. The wheels made a peculiar creaking noise that Edith said was called "the song of the axle." The oxen, yoked so they pulled the carts with their powerful heads and necks, plodded along, ignoring the commotion around them.

Then a sound like an admiring "ahhh" went up from the crowd and Trish saw why. The horses and riders were coming, the horses not merely walking but dancing with the excitement of the crowds and music. The horses were decorated with silver on their bridles and saddles, colorful hangings covering their chests and flanks, bells jangling, riders costumed as dashing conquistadors.

One horse and rider was less glitteringly attired than the others, but the magnificence of the horse and the rider's aristocratic stature made them stand out. Trish caught her breath. Marc and Demonio! The procession halted and Demonio, his head high, looked around contemptuously, like a king surveying the peasants. A dog started to yap at his heels, thought better of it, and retreated to tease a less dangerous target. Marc sat on the powerful horse with the ease of a born horseman, his expert hands keeping the highly-strung animal under control. His dark eyes were shadowed by the wide brim of his low-crowned black hat.

Trish inspected him freely from her safely anonymous position on the crowded stand. The children were looking up at Marc and the majestic stallion with a kind of awe. Trish tried not to feel it too, to remind herself that he was just another man, but she might have been looking back into time at some conquering aristocrat.

Suddenly her heart pounded as she realized her position was not so anonymous after all. Marc's head turned in her direction and his eyes caught hers. A faint smile curved his sensuous mouth and he touched his hat slightly in salute. Trish nodded in recognition. The parade resumed its forward progress but the chestnut stallion pranced to the side, children scattering in all directions.

Trish could now see the dark eyes under the shadowy brim, a light dancing in them that both thrilled and dismayed her. What did he want? He was making his way toward her, the dancing stallion held like a wound spring ready to uncoil.

"Señorita!" he greeted her with a flashing smile.

She dipped her head in acknowledgement, aware everyone was looking at them. Suddenly a powerful arm shot out and encircled her shoulders, pulling her toward him. Trish's lips parted as she looked into his darkly handsome face and laughing eyes. And then, before she could protest, his mouth met hers in a kiss that sent her heart hammering and her mind spinning. She was dimly aware that people were applauding around them. Trish clutched the rough seat for support as Marc touched his hat in salute and then galloped forward to take his place

145

in the parade. For a moment pure fury flooded through Trish. How dare he make a spectacle of her, using her to entertain the crowd like the silly antics of the clown, everyone watching, smiling, applauding as if it were some sort of amusing sideshow.

"Don't look now, but you're the envy of every unmarried girl present. And probably half the married ones too!" Edith whispered.

Trish drew a shaky breath and glanced around, suddenly realizing it would be better to laugh off the incident than to let anyone know how deeply it had affected her. She smiled and waved and people eventually turned back to watching the colorful parade. But Trish hardly saw anything. All she could see were those laughing, dancing eyes; all she could feel was herself melting under his kiss, the taste of his mouth on hers.

Edith had to nudge her when the parade was over. "I'm going to see if Armando has arrived with the fireworks yet. Would you like to come with me?"

"I think I'll just wander around and look at everything," Trish demurred. She didn't want to admit, even to herself, that she was hoping to see Marc.

Edith gave Trish a glance that was both sympathetic and concerned. "Don't expect too much," she said hesitantly. "Marc can be

146

devastatingly charming when he's interested in a woman, but he can also be . . . unfeeling when he tires of her."

Unfeeling. Translate that ruthless and cruel, Trish thought to herself, but all she said was a light, "I can take care of myself."

Edith went looking for Armando, and Trish wandered through the colorful crowd thronging the street. Booths selling food had been set up. The clown bounced around on a comically sad burro. Something exploded near Trish's ear, freezing her motionless for a moment in memory of a similar noise, until she realized it was only a harmless balloon popped by some overexuberant youngster. Now that was enough of that, she told herself firmly. She wasn't going to let every little noise send her into a frightened dither.

Trish wandered on, enjoying it all. She paused to watch a contest of children exhibiting their pets, everything from a recalcitrant pig to a parrot chattering loudly in Spanish. It was like a county fair back in Minnesota, she thought a bit breathlessly. She paused again, surprised and delighted to find a puppet show in progress. The dialogue was all in Spanish, too rapid for her to understand, but the slapstick action was humorous in any language.

Suddenly she saw a tall figure striding

147

along the street, his head moving above the crowd as if he were looking for someone. Through a break in the crowd she saw that he had changed his clothes, that he was now wearing the more familiar tan pants, boots, and expensive shirt carelessly open at the throat.

She stood stock still, fighting the urge to call his name. Then his dark eyes settled on her and he pushed his way toward her. She tried to quiet the singing of her heart, but it was like trying to quiet a chattering bird. He had been looking for her!

He tilted his head quizzically to one side, his dark eyes appraising. "Angry?"

"I should be."

He stood there, arrogantly sure of himself, a look of lazy amusement on his face. "If you aren't too angry to eat, I'll buy you some lunch," he offered.

For a moment Trish hesitated, remembering the doubts that had assailed her a few mornings ago. His knowledge of the horse's insane fear of gunshots, the opportunity to use that knowledge . . . .

"You're looking very serious," he commented with a raised brow. "No one is serious at fiesta time."

Knowledge and opportunity but no reason, she reminded herself firmly as she eyed his lean figure lounging carelessly against the puppet stand. Lack of a reason made any suspicions of him preposterous.

"I'm just trying to decide if I care to eat lunch with a man who goes around embarrassing innocent maidens," she said tartly.

His eyebrow rose again. "That was an innocent kiss?"

Trish flushed, remembering how she had responded to his embrace. He stepped closer and lifted her chin with his finger, the teasing laughter in his eyes replaced by a searing intensity. The crowd flowed around them unnoticed.

"That kiss was only the beginning," he said softly. "We'll finish it later."

His physical effect on her was instantaneous, as always, and she knew she would have melted into his arms right there on the crowded street. But he supported her with a bracing hand on her arm, his voice casual when he repeated, "Now, about that lunch?"

They ate *empañadas*, delicious little meat pies, washed down with a *refresco* of fresh tangerine juice and a mango-flavored sherbert for dessert. Trish had an unfamiliar, heady feeling that seemed to intensify each of her senses, though when Marc walked with her hand tucked through the crook of his elbow, she was conscious of little else but the feel of his powerful body next to hers.

After eating they watched the children's contests and games, laughed at contestants vainly trying to climb a greased pole and grab the money prize stationed at the top. Trish applauded when a slim little girl suddenly darted forward and captured the coveted prize, much to the chagrin of the perspiring young men. Marc shook his head in mock exasperation at this turn of events.

After that came the bullfights. At first Trish protested that she did not want to see them, never having approved of the torment and killing of an innocent animal in the guise of sport or entertainment. But Costa Rican bullfights, she found out, were different.

There was one bull but many *toreros* with capes. And there was no killing.

The arena was set up around a pool of water with a pole in the middle. The bull seemed to have the best of the game. The bullfighters usually wound up seeking sanctuary in the pool, and if the bull was unusually angry or the bullfighter exceptionally frightened, there was sometimes a hasty climb up the pole. The bullfight ended when the bull lost interest and became bored with chasing people. Then another bull was run in until

150

eventually everyone was too exhausted to continue. Trish left that contest approving of the Costa Rican idea of how to conduct a bullfight – so that both human and animal participants lived to enjoy another day.

There was only one less-than-enjoyable incident that happy afternoon. Someone had set up a shooting gallery with targets cut from shiny tin cans. Marc looked inquiringly at Trish as they sauntered past. Long ago Trish had shot at the crows that robbed her grandfather's garden. Now she shrugged and picked up one of the small guns, knocking over a fairly respectable seven out of ten tin-can targets. Then Marc picked up the gun, aimed quickly and expertly, and in quick succession hit all ten targets. He nodded at the proprietor to set the targets up again and just as quickly downed all ten again.

Trish watched, dismayed, her muscles tensing nervously. One of the deeper cuts from that fall into the mountain crater suddenly began to throb painfully. Marc obviously knew how to handle a gun efficiently and expertly. And just as obvious was his deadly accuracy. Again that unwanted thought: Marc knew about the gelding's violent reaction to the sound of gunshots. . . .

"Such a frown," Marc chided lightly as he

handed the gun back to the proprietor of the stand. "I didn't know you were such a poor loser."

Trish managed a noncommittal reply, but the incident left her with an unpleasant aftertaste. She wished they had never gone near the shooting gallery. She tried to push the thought out of her mind, reminding herself of how illogical and preposterous it was to be suspicious of Marc, but her uneasy doubts remained. Charming and exciting as Marc was, what did she really know about him except that he had a ruthless obsession with reuniting the two parts of the *cafetal* into one again, that deep-down he felt he had a hereditary right to the property, and that he could be ruthless where women were concerned?

"I haven't seen Edith all afternoon," Trish finally said uneasily. "Perhaps I should go and find her."

"If you wish. Perhaps she will join us for the *asado*."

Asado. Oh, yes, the barbecue for which Marc supplied the meat, Trish remembered.

They strolled around, even walking over to the car, but saw nothing of Edith until Marc spotted her helping Armando set up the evening fireworks display on the far side of the village soccer field. Armando was evidently trying to show Edith how to do something, and from the impatient way he stood with hands on hips, he was exasperated at her lack of understanding.

"Shall we go and offer our assistance?" Marc asked dryly.

Trish had to laugh, knowing he was not serious and knowing also what sort of reaction such an improbable offer would bring from Armando. "Some other time," she said lightly.

They returned to the main street then. The evening air cooled rapidly as the sun went down, but the crowd's enthusiasm and exuberance seemed to provide their own warmth. Marc and Trish (she seemed to be accepted as his partner for the moment) were served first from the *asado*. The meat was succulent roast pork, and there were tasty beans and rice, salads, and more cool, refreshing sherbet for dessert. Sitting in the place of honor with Marc, Trish did not see either Edith or Armando come through the line of hungry eaters. She wasn't really surprised. Armando would probably rather starve than eat anything provided by Marc.

Then came the music and dancing, first an exhibition of swirling-skirted girls and dashing young men whirling through an intricate series of local dances. Afterward

153

everyone danced to the rhythmic beat, though Marc did not seem interested in taking part. He merely sat, nodding approvingly now and then or calling a compliment to some smiling couple dancing by. He seemed relaxed, but now and then Trish thought she detected a hint of impatience in his solid grip on her hand.

Finally he glanced down at her, the torchlights set up to illuminate the street flickering in his dark eyes. "Tired?" he asked lightly.

"A little." She smiled. "But happy."

He stood up, pulling her with him. Unobtrusively, talking and greeting people as they moved along the street, Marc effectively worked their way to the edge of the crowd, his grip on Trish dragging her firmly with him.

"Wait!" Trish cried breathlessly, struggling to keep up. "What are we doing? Where are we going?"

He didn't answer. He pushed her into the dark, empty shadows behind the viewing stand. He cupped her face in his hands, his fingers tangled in her hair, and Trish's heart pounded with the suddenness and intensity of the caress. Her back was to the street and the torchlights flickered on his face, emphasizing its lean, aristocratic lines, but revealing something far more basic, something almost savagely male as he looked down at her.

"That kiss this morning was fine for amusing the spectators," he said, his voice deceptively soft. His fingers trailed a burning path across her cheek and lips. Then his voice turned almost harsh as he added, "But now I'm going to show you how it should be done."

Chapter Seven

Marc's mouth crushed down on hers, almost violent with pent-up passion. His hands holding her face slid down to encircle her body, pinning her arms against her sides, arching her slim body against the taut, muscular length of his. His mouth moved against hers deeply, roughly.

Trish responded with the same wild passion, to a depth of feeling no man had ever aroused in her before. Her closed eyes and pounding pulse shut out the sights and sounds around her. She was aware only of Marc's hard body holding her close, of a wild, soaring-in-space feeling. His hands moved across her back in a harsh yet sensual caress. Her arms strained to encircle his lean waist.

All day had been leading up to this moment,

Trish thought, as his mouth slid down to trail kisses along her exposed throat. This morning's brief, public kiss, all the touches, the glances, all merely preliminaries to this passionate moment. And now she knew what that unfamiliar, heady feeling she had had all day meant: She was falling in love.

She was trembling when he finally released her. There was a satisfied twist to the sensuous lips, as if knowing how he affected her pleased him. For a moment she was angry, but then she saw the faint tremor at the corner of his mouth and realized that his composure took more effort than he was willing to acknowledge.

"My car is over there," he said, motioning with one hand, the other firm on her arm. "Beyond those houses."

He took it for granted that she was leaving with him, and for one impetuous moment Trish was willing to abandon everything and follow him. Then she pulled back.

"I can't, Marc. I really can't!" she said breathlessly.

He turned to look at her again, and Trish knew he was frowning, though she couldn't see his handsome face clearly. They were even farther away from the flickering torches now, and only the planes and angles of his face were visible, his eyes in dark shadows. He seemed to be calculating, weighing something in his mind.

Then, without speaking, he reached for her again, slowly, deliberately. He pulled her body against his, not explosively or violently now, but almost leisurely, as if he had all the time in the world. He molded their bodies together and his kiss was as passionate as before, but different ... the difference between a flash fire, quickly extinguished, and smoldering coals ignited into a never-ending, all-consuming flame. Butterfly kisses on her eyelids, feathery caresses of his lips on her temples, tantalizing nibbles at the corner of her mouth all left her weak and trembling.

Trish felt as if she were melting in his arms, devoid of willpower, logic, or rational thought. A liquid fire coursed through her veins. Finally he stepped back, his hands still gripping her shoulders as she swayed unsteadily.

"That ... that isn't fair," she said weakly, almost resentful of the power he had over her, feeling somehow manipulated by his expertise. He laughed softly and Trish's anger flared. "You did that on purpose!"

"Would you prefer I made love to you without purpose? Merely a pleasant way to pass the time of day, perhaps?"

Trish's teeth caught her lower lip, full and

swollen with the passion of his kisses. She felt bewildered and uncertain, doubtful of his feelings toward her. One minute he seemed on the verge of returning her awakening love, but a moment later she felt he was only toying with her, amusing himself with arousing her to melting helplessness. She remembered what he had said earlier in the day: "No one is serious at fiesta time."

She was falling in love with him, deeply, passionately in love, but perhaps this was all just a fiesta game with him, an exhibition of his skill in the game of love in the same way his downing the targets had exhibited his skill in that area.

Trish took a shaky breath. "Edith would be hurt and Armando furious if I didn't stay for the fireworks display he has worked so hard on."

"I see." Marc's voice was cool. "You seem very concerned about Armando's feelings."

"Edith and I came together in her car and it would be rude to desert her and leave her to drive home alone."

"Of course." Now he sounded as remote as the mountain looming in the night sky behind him.

Trish opened her mouth, ready to throw courtesy and Edith's feelings and Armando's anger to the winds to erase that remote indifference in his voice and reverse the feeling of withdrawal she sensed in him.

But he didn't give her the opportunity. He touched her elbow, firmly but impersonally turning her back toward the crowded street. "I'll escort you to the fireworks display."

If Trish thought that meant he intended to stay and view the display with her, she was mistaken. He took her to the edge of the field where others were now also gathering in anticipation.

"You should have a good view from here," he remarked, as impersonal as a theater usher guiding a moviegoer to a seat. "Thank you for an enjoyable afternoon."

Trish looked up at him, her lips parted. Her first impulse was to apologize, but then she pressed her lips together angrily. She had done nothing for which to apologize. If anyone should apologize it should be Marc for attempting to seduce her into being rude to her hosts.

She lifted her head and said with cool dignity, "I enjoyed it too."

He turned and departed then, and her eyes reluctantly followed his tall figure threading through the crowd. At the end he hadn't seemed so much angry with her as merely resigned. She almost wished he had yelled and railed at her. Anything would have been better than this aloof, impersonal indifference. It made her feel again that he had tried to manipulate and use her, and when he had failed, he had simply shrugged and cut her adrift.

She examined her own feelings again. Had she really been so concerned about Edith's and Armando's feelings? Or had she been afraid of her own feelings, the subconscious knowledge that her body, not her mind, was in control around Marc? No, it was more than that, more than just physical desire. She was falling in love with him, plunging uncontrollably with mind, soul, and body.

The fireworks interrupted her tremulous self-examination with a burst of glittering blue and gold, calculated to catch everyone's attention. In quick succession explosions of red and sparkling silver, fountains of trailing stars and glowing sunbursts followed. Then came a rather long, unexplained delay. Some people started to drift away, thinking the display was over, but then the bursts began again, bringing ahs from the adults and squeals from the children. Trish had to smile when one firework gave a harmless whoosh and fizzled to the ground, and the audience laughed. Armando would be furious. Trish knew him well enough to realize he thought of this as a dramatic presentation, not something

160

to be laughed at. The grand finale, also slow in coming, was a ground display of sizzling fireworks that in the afterglow left the burning image of the Costa Rican flag.

Afterward Trish wandered around pretending to look at the displays again but really watching for Marc. Disappointed, she saw no sign of his commanding figure. Evidently he had left. He was behaving like a pouting child, she told herself angrily. But she had only to remember the passion of those kisses to realize he was no child.

Finally Trish crossed the makeshift soccer field to where Edith and Armando were still moving around, flashlights bobbing. Armando appeared to be setting up some sort of complicated display for the next evening's performance. Edith was gathering used materials into a trash box.

"It was a marvelous display," Trish called. "Congratulations."

"Armando is angry with me. He says I am all thumbs as an assistant." Edith laughed, but it was a nervous sound and she sent Armando an uneasy glance.

"Or feet," he retorted sharply, humorlessly.

"Armando had a line of rockets set up to fire. I stumbled over them and caused a delay," Edith explained. "Perhaps you noticed."

161

"It wasn't all that noticeable," Trish assured her. "Everyone thought it was a fantastic display."

Armando was still working on the ground display, ignoring the two of them. Trish could see Edith watching him nervously out of the corner of her eye. With Armando in such ill humor over something so minor, it appeared to Trish that the best course of action was to leave him to stew by himself.

"If you're finished picking things up, perhaps we should start home," Trish suggested to Edith.

Edith looked relieved at the suggestion and nodded, but Armando grumbled something about needing some help yet.

"Of course," Edith said, her voice strained. "If you'll just explain to me what it is you want –"

"Trish, how about you? Are you all thumbs and feet?" Armando asked in a sarcastic tone.

Trish had no desire to stay and help Armando do anything, but one look at Edith's tense face made her say tentatively, "Well, if there's anything I could do to help –"

"Yes, why don't you stay and help Armando," Edith agreed, jumping on the idea with alacrity. "I'll run on home and have something ready to eat by the time the two of you get there."

162

Armando made no comment one way or the other. Trish leaned over and squeezed Edith's arm.

"Don't let it upset you. Men get these vile moods when things don't go to suit them," she whispered. Especially, she thought to herself as she heard Armando hit his finger and curse under his breath in Spanish, when it's their own fault and they blame someone else.

Edith left then, angling across the field to miss the crowded street where the marimba music was still going strong. Trish walked over to Armando.

"What can I do to help?"

"I'm going to do a special display from the top of that hill over there," Armando said. "You can help carry things in a minute."

Trish stood around on one foot and then the other, wishing she had brought a sweater. There was one in the car, but Edith had no doubt driven off with it by now. Finally Armando handed her a hammer and some string and told her to follow him. Trish was half annoyed, half amused. Certainly Armando could have carried those small additional items himself. He was annoyed with Edith's awkwardness, or his own shortcomings, and being childishly petulant.

There was supposed to be a trail up the hill, but the way branches slapped her in

163

the face and vines tangled around her feet, Trish had her doubts that they were on it. Panting, they finally arrived at the top. Trish was pleased to find the view, at least, well worth the trip. The entire village lay below them, the main street a riot of color and motion. From somewhere beyond the village came another strange glow. Trish watched it for a moment but couldn't identify it. Perhaps some revelers were having a private celebration, she decided.

Armando asked her to hold a couple of boards together while he nailed them. He explained that what he intended was to have Edith or Trish come up here and set this off as the finale, which would surprise everyone since they wouldn't be expecting anything from this direction. Trish thought privately that it would have made more sense to come up here in the daylight tomorrow and do this, but perhaps Armando was afraid someone would see and that would ruin the surprise.

Trish looked out over the village again before they started down. There seemed to be an unusual amount of activity and even shouts audible this far away. Perhaps that was the way a fiesta ended for the night, Trish decided.

Armando paused beside her. "I should not have been so abrupt with Edith, should I? She

164

was trying to help and I lost my temper," he said regretfully. Trish didn't comment and he added, "But I want to thank you for . . . for smoothing things over." Unexpectedly he reached for her hand and touched it to his lips.

Trish momentarily stiffened but there was nothing but gratitude mixed with apology on his face, and she felt guilty for even momentarily misinterpreting the gesture. Marc had manipulated her so skillfully with his kisses that now she was suspicious of any man's actions.

"Come," Armando said. "I must apologize to Edith."

They made better time going down the hill and headed back toward the original fireworks site. Armando said his pickup was parked there.

A man came running across the field toward them. "Señor! Señor Albéniz!"

Trish turned, alarmed by something in the man's voice. Armando strode out to meet him, asking a question in sharp Spanish.

The man's answer was rapid-fire. Trish cursed her limited Spanish, which always seemed to fail her just when she needed it most. But fear stabbed at her when she caught Edith's name and saw the roll of the man's eyes. He motioned toward the road and

165

with a sickening plunge of her stomach Trish remembered that peculiar glow she had seen.

"What is it?" she cried. "What has happened?"

Armando turned back to her. "There has been an accident. Edith's car. He does not know how badly she is injured or if –"

He didn't finish the awful thought. *Or if she is dead.* The tools, the fireworks, everything was forgotten, abandoned as Armando ran to the pickup. Trish barely had time to slide into the passenger's side before he hurtled the pickup out of the concealing thicket, careening wildly over shrubs and vines. Trish could see that the street was emptying as people thronged down the road. Armando used the horn, hardly slowing for the pedestrians, and they shoved and fell over one another getting out of his way. Trish knew she yelled something at him but he didn't seem to hear.

The glow grew as they rounded one steep, twisting curve after another, and then it was no longer a glow but a leaping mountain of flame. Within the flames could be seen the gaunt framework of what had once been a car.

"Oh, my God!" Trish breathed in horror.

Armando seemed too stunned and shocked even to speak. He stopped dead in the middle of the road and his hands gripped the wheel as

166

though frozen there. He stared at the leaping tongues as if transfixed.

Trish was dimly aware that someone was pounding on the window on Armando's side. She touched him, and reached across him to roll the window down when he seemed too numbed to respond.

The man rattled something in rapid Spanish. Again Trish felt helpless, but Armando stirred, then barked a question in reply. The man smiled and nodded with an eager "*Sí!*"

Armando turned back to Trish. "Edith isn't in there." He reached in his pocket and ran a handkerchief with shaky hands across his forehead. "Someone got her out before the car burst into flames."

"Thank God."

Trish leaned back limply, her head thrown back on the seat, but her relief was short-lived, as Armando went on to say that Edith was injured, no one seemed to know how seriously, and one of the other *cafetal* owners was taking her directly to a San José hospital.

Armando didn't ask if Trish wanted to go along. He didn't look back as they left the burning car, the flames beginning to die down now. Armando drove without talking, almost as if he had forgotten that Trish was even beside him.

167

It was a wild ride, but Trish knew nothing she could say would slow Armando down. She gritted her teeth and held on, trying not to think of that mangled, flaming car behind them. What had happened? Edith was a cautious driver, experienced on these steep, winding roads. Perhaps a disastrous attempt to avoid some wild animal crossing the road?

"It was my fault." Armando's low, agonized voice interrupted her thoughts. "I was cross with her. I hurt her feelings and she is sensitive. It is my fault!"

"Armando, no," Trish protested, but suddenly she couldn't put any authority into her voice. Edith had been upset when she left the fiesta. A curve taken too fast while her mind was elsewhere.

"She was upset. She drove too fast, too carelessly," Armando said, putting Trish's thoughts into words. "And all because of me, because of the stupid things I said." He burst into a torrent of self-berating Spanish.

Trish patted his arm helplessly. "Isn't there someplace closer than San José where they could have taken her?"

Armando didn't answer, his thoughts evidently turning inward again. Trish slumped back, wishing Marc were here with his strength and assurance. Her earlier annoyance with him was gone in her desperate

168

need for him now.

They reached the outskirts of San José. Armando took a different route from the one Trish and Marc had taken to the city. Within minutes they pulled into the brightly lit emergency entrance of a hospital. Armando slammed out of the pickup and ran for the door, not waiting for Trish.

Inside, several people were milling around. Trish vaguely recognized them as people to whom she had been introduced earlier in the day, but she could recall no names. The conversation was all in Spanish, much to Trish's frustration, though she understood enough to gather Edith had been taken into emergency surgery.

At least she wasn't dead.

It was a blurred, unreal night. Edith came out of surgery but was in Intensive Care. She had broken her arm, the jagged end of the bone protruding through the skin. She also had head injuries and there was the possibility of internal damage. Armando walked around too dazed to communicate, muttering to himself. He angrily brushed away Trish's attempts to soothe him and ease his torment over the unkind things he had said to Edith.

The next morning Edith was finally taken to a regular hospital room. She was still heavily sedated, however, and the doctor suggested it would be evening before they could talk with her. Armando seemed too distracted to know what to do next, and Trish gently suggested that perhaps they could find rooms nearby and get some rest. He nodded and Trish gave him a gentle push toward the door while she went back to ask if there was anything they should bring for Edith that evening.

A moment later she was glad Armando had gone out to the pickup because Marc walked in the other door. Trish moved toward him and felt herself swaying. All night she had been the strong, efficient one, filling out forms, answering questions, reassuring Armando. But she had been surviving on sheer willpower these last few hours, and now that Marc was here all she wanted was the secure strength of his arms around her. Coming through the door he looked like a solid rock of strength, his step firm, his clothes crisp and fresh. Her steps toward him quickened.

"Marc!" she breathed gladly. "It's so good to see –"

"I came as soon as I heard." He put out his arms, but not to embrace her. His hands on her upper arms held her lightly but firmly at a distance. His dark eyes looking down at her

170

were remote, his expression impassive.

Trish was momentarily puzzled, then angry. "You're not still angry about last night, are you?" she gasped.

"I beg your pardon?"

Trish just stared at him, angry and dismayed that he would let their trivial disagreement of the previous night come between them at a time like this. But his eyes met hers challengingly and there was no retreat in his gaze.

Trish dropped her arms and stepped away from him. He made no effort to restrain her. Crisply she explained what little she knew about the accident and Edith's condition.

He raised a dark eyebrow. "I understood you planned to ride home with Edith."

"Armando asked me to stay and help him set up a fireworks display. He and Edith had a little . . . disagreement. Now he's blaming himself for upsetting her and causing the accident." Trish deliberately kept her voice neutral, as unemotional as possible, trying to regather her strength after almost coming apart with relief when Marc arrived.

"I see. Has Edith's father been informed."

Trish bit her lip, aghast. Never once had she given even a moment's thought to Edith's father. The servants might have told him, but somehow Trish doubted that, considering his

171

uncertain physical condition. She shook her head.

"I'll take care of it then," he said authoritatively.

For a moment Trish was startled, but then she remembered that at one time Marc and Robert Hepler had been cooperating neighbors – though Marc, no doubt, had ulterior motives and intended to use the friendship to get hold of the *cafetal* someday, she thought caustically.

"I'm sure Edith would appreciate that," Trish said.

"Is there anything I can do . . . for Edith?" he added pointedly.

"I don't think so. We may be able to see her this evening, but I'm not even sure about that."

"And what are your plans?"

Briefly she explained that she and Armando planned to find temporary rooms nearby. He listened without comment and thanked her as impersonally as if she were a hospital employee giving out information. Her eyes followed him as he strode away without looking back, her feelings a turmoil of anger, dismay, and heartache. *Damn him!* she thought furiously, acting like a petulant child because he didn't get his way. Or had she been the child, playing with passion like some fumbling adolescent? Oh, but there was nothing childish or adolescent about her feelings, she thought with a wrench of pain. Even after his rebuff, his cold indifference, she was still falling in love with him. In fact, she thought with despair, it was too late for that. She *was* in love with him.

Dispiritedly she went out the other way and found Armando waiting in the pickup. He seemed to have slid into the seat, placed his hands on the wheel, and not moved since. Trish made no mention of having seen Marc.

They ate a silent meal and then found rooms at an adequate, though hardly luxurious hotel. Trish washed her face, too weary even for a bath, pulled the drapes, and fell into bed.

It was late afternoon when she woke to an insistent tapping on the door. It was Armando, suggesting they have something to eat and then go to the hospital as soon as possible. Trish agreed. She hurried through a shower, wrinkling her nose distastefully at the soiled, wilted clothing she had to put back on.

Armando seemed to have revived somewhat. He looked less like a zombie, although he couldn't seem to get his mind off the idea that he was responsible for the accident. At the hospital, the doctor gave permission for a short visit. Anxious as Trish was to see Edith, she suggested that Armando go in first, knowing he and Edith would want a few minutes alone. She waited in the hall, pacing back and forth, until Armando came to the door and beckoned to her.

Trish steeled herself for the worst when she stepped inside the door, but it was not as bad as she feared. Edith's head and arm were bandaged and her smile a bit tremulous, but she was smiling. A tangle of tubes and bottles surrounded the bed.

Trish started to reach for her, then pulled back. "I want to hug you but I don't know where without hurting you!"

Edith turned her palm up and Trish squeezed it emotionally. "We're certainly a pair of accident-prone ones, aren't we?" she said huskily. "Is there anything I can do?"

"I don't think so." Edith looked at Armando, her plain face soft and glowing with love. "Except maybe convince Armando that it wasn't his fault. I was upset, but that had nothing to do with the accident."

"I could kill myself for the stupid things I said," Armando muttered remorsefully.

"Edith, what did happen?" Trish asked.

Edith's brow wrinkled, then she winced as the movement evidently brought pain from her stitched scalp wounds. "I don't know.

174

I didn't notice anything unusual when I got into the car and drove off. But by the second or third turn the brakes felt rather soft, as if they weren't pushing against anything. And then the car just went out of control and there were no brakes at all. I made it around the first few turns, but the car kept picking up speed. And then —"

Her voice broke off, momentary terror filling her eyes until Armando touched her reassuringly. Trish stood up, quickly realizing this couldn't be doing Edith any good. With a final squeeze of Edith's hand, Trish left them alone to say their good-byes.

Outside the door she paced back and forth again, thinking about what Edith had said. Was this just an accident or was it another in a sinister chain of events? Was there any connection among all these "accidents"? Could someone have deliberately tampered with the brakes? And why was Edith a target now, after the other "accidents" had been aimed at Trish?

The questions hurtled through Trish's mind like projectiles, bewildering, unanswerable. Then another thought came: Perhaps Edith was not meant to be the target after all. Trish was supposed to be in that car, had planned to be in it until almost the very last moment. Was it possible the victim was supposed to be Trish? And that someone was ruthlessly willing to let Edith die too, if she happened to be in the car, just to get Trish.

Trish leaned against the wall for support, her legs suddenly weak at the horror of that thought. Someone utterly ruthless, utterly obsessed . . .

If nothing else, she thought shakily, this eliminated any last, lingering doubts she might have about Robert Hepler. Even if, by some wild stretch of the imagination, he could have tampered with the car, he would never have risked injuring his own daughter. He might hate Trish passionately, but he would never harm Edith. Having observed the closeness between them, Trish could not doubt that.

Anyone could have known Trish was supposed to be in that car, Trish reflected – the servants, the *cafetal* owners they had talked with at the fiesta, maybe someone who simply hated gringos.

But she knew those were all unlikely suspicions. She tried to convince herself that the other lurking suspicion was just as unlikely, but it wouldn't go away.

Marc knew she was supposed to be in that car. He had even questioned her about it this morning.

Preposterous, she told herself firmly. Absurd.

Armando came out of the room. Edith had requested that they pick up a few toilet articles for her and he was eager to comply. Without so much as a toothbrush along, Trish needed some things also.

The following morning they learned that Edith would be hospitalized for a week. By now it appeared there were no serious internal injuries. Edith said she could get along fine, that she did not want to cause anyone inconvenience, but Trish stayed in San José to be near her. Armando took care of his responsibilities at the plantation during the mornings and drove into San José in the afternoons.

One day he brought in a letter that had arrived for Trish from her mother. It was an odd letter, Trish thought, not totally disapproving of what she had done in coming here but rather distant, with something of an I-wash-my-hands-of-this-matter attitude. She did, however, send her love to Edith, and Trish passed that on. Edith seemed pleased. In fact, she opened up somewhat and talked about memories of their mother, a lovely birthday party her mother had once arranged, how broken up her father had been when their mother left him.

Trish admired the way Edith managed to remain cheerful, even to make light of her injuries. Edith remarked that if the cast on her arm was not removed before the wedding, at least the white color would blend with her white wedding gown. She suggested that if her hair hadn't grown out by then that she would just have to get a wig.

"I wonder how I'd look as a blonde?" she mused, and they both laughed.

In Edith's presence Trish kept up a gay good humor too, but alone she couldn't escape her dismal feelings about her last meeting with Marc. Nor could she escape her brooding suspicions. Finally she decided there was one thing she must do to set her mind at ease. She brought up the subject as she and Armando left the hospital together one afternoon.

"Armando, has it ever struck you as peculiar that the brakes on the car went out so suddenly that night?" she began. "I know they were working all right when Edith and I drove to the village earlier in the day."

Armando cocked his dark head. "I have been so worried about Edith that I have thought of little else. But, now that you mention this, it did happen rather abruptly, didn't it? But perhaps that is the way brakes are." He shrugged ruefully. "Unfortunately

178

my knowledge of the automobile is rather limited."

"Mine too. But there's something I think we should do." She paused beside the Mercedes Armando had driven into San José that day. "I think we should inspect the car. Or what is left of it anyway. Do you know where it is?"

He shook his head doubtfully. "I told one of the men in the village to take a cable and pull it out of the ravine. He has probably taken it to a junkyard by now."

"But you aren't sure?" she pursued. When he shook his head, she went on rapidly. "Then let's go to the village today and see if we can look at it. I'll stay at the *cafetal* tonight and ride back to San José with you tomorrow. We won't mention anything to Edith."

"But why?" He looked perplexed. "What would we be looking for?"

"I don't know," Trish admitted. Her knowledge of the mechanical workings of an automobile was probably even more limited than Armando's. "To see if we can find anything that had been cut, broken, or tampered with in some way, I guess."

"Trish, what are you suggesting?" Armando asked slowly, his eyes widening. "That someone deliberately –"

"No, not really," Trish said hastily. "I just
179

want to make sure in my own mind that it really was an accident." She hesitated. "There have been so many accidents."

Armando's face darkened grimly as he glanced upward in the direction of Edith's room. "Have you mentioned any of this to Edith?"

Trish shook her head. "I didn't want to alarm her."

He nodded approvingly, but his face was set and grim as he held the car door open for Trish. "Come, we must not waste any more time."

Chapter Eight

Trish forced herself not to look the other way when they passed the burned area where the car had gone up in flames. The ground was blackened, the surrounding trees and brush scorched. She thought briefly about asking Armando to stop there but decided there was no point in it. If anything could be learned, it would be from the mangled car itself.

The village was quiet when they entered, far different from the day of the fiesta. Odd, Trish thought now, but she had hardly thought of the fiesta after that fateful day. Had it continued as usual, as though nothing had happened, the patron saint solemnly returned to his usual place after the annual sojourn to the spring. There were still some marks on the ground where the temporary grandstand had stood, and Trish's heart lurched unexpectedly as she remembered what had happened there. Had Marc returned to the fiesta to bestow his kisses on someone else? She had neither seen nor heard from him since his cold visit to the hospital the morning after the accident.

Armando drove the length of the dusty street. A few children looked at them curiously and waved. A chicken, scratching industriously in the road, squawked and fluttered out of the way.

"There!" Trish cried suddenly, spotting a tangle of blackened metal behind one of the houses.

"You have sharp eyes," Armando commented approvingly.

He parked the car on the edge of the street and they walked around the house. Trish stared at the burned skeleton in dismay. She had no idea where to start looking or what to look for, nor, staring at the gaunt frame, any real hope that anything positive would be revealed. She touched a door tentatively, with the eerie feeling that she wouldn't have been surprised to find it still hot. It wasn't, of course, but her fingers came away blackened. Armando poked at what had once been the engine, now bent and melted into a tangled mass.

"I don't think the brakes are up there, are they?" Trish asked doubtfully.

Armando lifted his shoulders helplessly. "I just don't know where to look. I know about growing coffee and bananas, but cars . . . ?" He shook his head.

Trish nodded, feeling vaguely let down. What had she hoped to find? Proof that the car had been tampered with? No. Deep down she wanted proof that this was all some terrible accident, proof that would stop the awful suspicions gnawing at her mind. But she doubted that this blackened mass could reveal anything.

"Señor Albéniz!"

They both looked up as a man approached from the house, talking rapidly in Spanish. As usual, Trish lagged behind in translating what he was saying to Armando, but she gathered he was apologizing about something. He looked relieved when Armando assured him everything was all right.

"He says he is sorry that the car is still here, but he has not had time to dispose of it yet," Armando explained. "I told him I was pleased

182

that it was still here."

"Does he know anything about cars?" Trish asked.

The man nodded eagerly, evidently understanding enough English so that he did not need to wait for Armando's translation. "*Mecánico*," he said proudly.

"He's a mechanic at the *beneficio*," Armando explained. "He helps keep our trucks in good running order."

Slowly and carefully Trish used her limited Spanish to ask the mechanic if he could tell what had caused the brakes to fail. Without hesitating he crawled partway under the car. Trish and Armando knelt to peer at the broken length of tubing he pointed out to them.

"What is that?" Trish questioned.

The answer came back through Armando's translation. "He says that is the brake line. It supplies the fluid to the brakes. If the line is broken, all the fluid leaks out and you have no brakes."

Which was exactly what had happened to Edith, Trish thought slowly. Again she directed a question to the mechanic, asking him if the broken line was the result of natural wear and tear or if it could have been deliberately cut.

The man frowned and inspected the

183

blackened, bent tube again. He looked at Trish as if he might attempt to answer her directly, but finally he launched into a long and seemingly complicated explanation to Armando in Spanish. Trish listened in frustration, understanding only enough to be tantalized and swearing to herself that she was going to master this language so thoroughly that she would never again be at a loss.

Finally the man crawled out. Armando stood up and wiped his hands on his handkerchief.

"He says the brake line could have been damaged at some time in the past, perhaps bent by hitting something. Then over a period of time it worked back and forth until it eventually broke."

"Then it was just an accident!" Trish said, relief surging through her.

Armando shook his head. "Not necessarily. He doubts that the brake line was actually cut with some tool, but he says the tube could have been severed by being deliberately bent back and forth until it broke."

The mechanic nodded. To illustrate he picked up a stray piece of wire from the ground and rapidly bent it back and forth a few times until it snapped in two.

Trish looked at the two pieces of broken wire, her heart sinking. "Done by someone who was careful enough to try to make it look as though it could have been natural wear and tear," she said slowly.

Armando nodded. "I'm afraid so. It's a frightening thought, isn't it?"

He turned back to the mechanic and thanked him for his help. Trish added her *gracias*. Armando spoke a few more words in Spanish and then motioned Trish back to the Mercedes.

"You told him to dispose of the car, didn't you?" Trish's smooth brow creased slightly. "Do you think that was wise?"

"I don't think I could stand to look at the cursed thing every time I came to the village," Armando admitted with a shudder. "It makes me feel sick just to look at it. I still feel that if I had not behaved so . . . so like an ass toward Edith, none of this would have happened. If her mind had not been distracted by what I said, she might have noticed the brake problem earlier, in time to prevent the accident.

Trish nodded but was not really paying attention to his words because another thought had just occurred to her. She turned back to the mechanic and put a detaining hand on Armando's arm. "Ask him if anyone else has been here to inspect the car," she directed Armando.

The answer came back loud and clear. Marcantonio de la Barca had come to look at the car even before it was pulled out of the ravine. However, the mechanic added, he himself had not been around when the *señor* inspected the burned car and he did not know whether or not the broken brake line had been noticed. Trish had no doubts but that Marc had noticed. Was he checking to see if his dirty work had been concealed by the fire? But why? Why?

Armando looked at her with concern after they slid into the Mercedes from opposite sides. "Trish, my dear, you look frightened."

"I . . . I guess I am," Trish admitted with a shaky smile. "First the fire in my room, then the gunshots when I was riding the horse. Now this. That's a lot of accidents."

Armando frowned. "But I do not see the connection. If you were the one injured in the car wreck, yes, it would truly seem suspicious. But –"

"But don't you remember? I was supposed to be in that car!" Trish cried. "I'm afraid Edith was almost killed because someone was trying to get me."

Armando looked dumbfounded and his hand halted halfway to the ignition key. His eyes, dark and troubled, met Trish's.

"I know it doesn't make any sense. I've

186

been over it in my mind a hundred times." Trish shook her head wearily. "I don't even know anyone here. I can't imagine why anyone would want to hurt me."

"But you asked if anyone else had come to look at the car," Armando said thoughtfully. "And you did not seem surprised to learn that Marcantonio de la Barca had been there before us."

Trish nodded. "But Marc has no reason –"

"Hasn't he?" Armando's voice was bitter. "I have been blind. I knew the man was not to be trusted, but I did not realize his obsession would lead him to such desperate acts."

"What do you mean?" Trish asked, alarm rising in her voice. All along she had been able to fight down her lurking suspicions of Marc as preposterous because there was no possible reason to warrant them, but now Armando's bitter voice suggested there was reason indeed.

Armando started the engine decisively. "I must think about this. I hope I am wrong."

He was silent and scowling all the way to the house, saying absentmindedly that he would meet her later for dinner. Trish went to her room. She had not been there since the night of the accident. All her things had been neatly put away, but the room, though familiar, also seemed foreign, as if

187

she had been away for months instead of a few days. She crossed to the window, her eyes automatically looking toward Marc's house. Like the room, it seemed oddly both familiar and foreign. Demonio paced his fence. A gardener trimmed the bougainvillea. Marc's Italian sports car waited in the driveway. All familiar and yet . . .

She turned away from the window, unexpectedly shivering. What was Armando thinking?

Trish undressed, first thinking about a dip in the pool but deciding against it and settling for a stinging shower instead. She composed a letter to send home, telling her mother about Edith's accident and injuries.

She was almost reluctant to go to the dining room at dinnertime, afraid of what she might hear. Her trepidation increased when she saw Armando standing by the window, a drink in one hand and a grim look on his face.

He turned. "May I fix you a drink?" he offered quickly.

Trish shook her head. Her stomach already felt distinctly jittery. She had almost given up smoking after the fire, but now she nervously fumbled in her purse for a cigarette. Armando moved swiftly to light it for her.

"What I have to say is not pleasant," he said grimly. "Perhaps after dinner . . .?"

188

Trish shook her head again. "I don't think I could eat."

Armando nodded briskly. "Very well then. Sit down." He paced back and forth along the dining room windows, stopped once to look directly at her. "I hope you will be able to keep an open mind and not let your personal feelings affect your judgment."

"I'll try," Trish said slowly, her palms already damp with dread.

"I think," Armando began directly, "that you have every reason to be afraid. I do not mean to frighten you unnecessarily, but we must face facts."

Trish nodded. Nervously she stubbed out the barely smoked cigarette. It tasted bitter and unpleasant in her mouth.

"You have had two unfortunate accidents," he began thoughtfully. "At first I truly believed they were accidents, although, after consideration, I must agree with your suspicion that they were not so accidental after all. Now you suspect that Edith's accident was also intentional and that someone, believing you would be in the car, caused it to happen with the idea of taking your life."

"I think that says it all in a nutshell," Trish agreed, trying to keep her voice light, but the words came out shaky instead.

A servant entered with steaming dishes, but

189

Armando waved her away. His eyes followed the woman thoughtfully, and he did not speak again until she was out of earshot. Trish wondered if he had awakened to another of her suspicions, that information passed freely from this household to the De la Barca household, either by accident or deliberately.

Armando's voice was lower when he spoke again. "But I believe there is one error in your thinking. You have perhaps looked at the situation backward."

A slightly puzzled frown creased Trish's forehead. "I don't understand what you mean."

Armando pulled out a chair beside her and sat down. "Let us look at each of these accidents. First the fire. It seemed obvious to me you had been smoking in bed. Edith told me you insisted the door was locked when you tried to get out, but –" He shook his head ruefully. "I am afraid I thought it was some silly schoolgirl imagining on your part."

Trish nodded. "That's what I finally told myself too."

"But consider this. Edith only recently moved to the other wing of the house to be near her father. Up until a few days before you arrived, the room in which you slept was Edith's room and had been for years. I'm sure anyone familiar with the household

190

knew that."

Trish nodded, still not understanding exactly what he was getting at.

"Then there was your accident with the horse, which I also assumed happened merely because of an unfortunate coincidence, because some careless hunter fired shots when you just happened to be riding a horse that was insanely afraid of gunshots. But consider this: Up until the last-minute change of plans, Edith was supposed to go on that ride. And you were wearing Edith's red hat, a hat everyone has seen and is familiar with."

Trish nodded again.

"And now, in the accident with the car, Edith herself was injured and would have died if it had not been for the quick action of our neighbor Señor Juárez, who managed to drag her out before the fire trapped her."

Armando's words spun in Trish's mind, slowing like a roulette wheel to settle into a particular slot from a circle of choices. "What you're saying," she said slowly, "is that someone was really after Edith all along. The only accident was that twice I was almost the victim instead. But this last time the . . . the assailant got Edith, the person he was really after all along."

Armando nodded. "Exactly. Except that he failed again," he said, his voice grim, "because Edith is still alive. Which means he will try again."

"But why?" Trish cried. "And who?"

Armando touched her hand lightly, almost sympathetically. "Do you really need to ask?" he asked gently.

Trish shook her head in protest. "No. There must be some other explanation."

"It is all so plain and I have been so blind." Armando sighed remorsefully. "If Marcantonio de la Barca can do away with Edith before she marries me, her father will sell the *cafetal* to him. It is as simple as that. And never doubt, dear, naive little Trish, that our neighbor is ruthless enough to kill to get what he wants."

Trish's mind twisted and turned to deny the truth of what Armando was saying. "But the fire . . . I don't see how Marc could possibly –"

"Don't you?" Armando looked at her compassionately. "Or is it because you do not want to see? Do you not think Marcantonio knows this house as well as he knows his own? Do you not think he knows in what room Edith has slept for years? That the key hangs just outside that room? He merely waited until a safe hour of the night when he was sure she slept, calmly placed the lit cigarette where he thought it would catch

192

the curtains, walked out, and locked the door behind him."

Something jarred in Trish's mind. "But Edith doesn't even smoke! Surely Marc would realize that a fire started by a cigarette in the room of someone who does not smoke would arouse suspicions!"

Armando smiled and shrugged lightly. "Ah, but she does smoke, though seldom where she can be seen. She does not consider it ladylike. Perhaps a holdover from the times her father locked her in that very room for punishment when he caught her smoking as a teenager."

Trish's mind felt numb but she couldn't accept what he was saying. No, she corrected herself despairingly, she didn't want to accept it. With one final flare of hope she protested, "But the servants said the door was not locked when they arrived."

Armando frowned and tapped the table thoughtfully with his empty glass. "I must admit this has puzzled me also. But I believe that Marcantonio cold-bloodedly waited outside the room until you tried to get out the door. When you abandoned the effort, he thought you . . . or Edith, actually . . . had been overcome by the smoke. Then he unlocked the door so it would truly appear Edith had been accidentally killed by smoke or fire. A locked door would surely have aroused suspicions, so he had to stay and unlock it to make the incident appear accidental."

And the key was right there, readily available, Trish thought hollowly. A key used to lock the door, unlock it again at the proper moment, and then quietly replaced on its nail.

She did not need to discuss with Armando the details of how the accident on the mountain had been handled. Marc undoubtedly knew, through information from the servants, that she and Edith planned to ride up Monte Decepción that day. He also knew, from having owned the horse himself, of the animal's violent reaction to gunshots. He climbed the mountain on foot, an easy enough task for someone in his superb physical condition, as she had already realized, and lay in wait. When only one rider arrived, he must have realized there had been some last-minute change in plans, but even in the concealing fog the floppy red hat had easily identified the lone rider as Edith. He had fired and disappeared into the mists, ready to be properly indignant when his caretaker informed him later at the office that the lathered horse had galloped in.

She remembered Marc's shock at seeing her scratched and bruised in the courtyard, the brooding look on his face when she opened her eyes. What had he been feeling? Anger that he had failed in his aim to do away with Edith? Remorse that he had almost killed Trish instead? Disgust that she had gotten in his way?

"Trish, I am sorry," Armando said. "Marcantonio can be very charming, very romantic. I know how you feel about him."

No, Trish thought despairingly, *Armando couldn't know*. What she felt was no dreamy, romantic infatuation. It was love, deep, powerful, and passionate. And totally unthinkable, beyond the bounds of reason or morality. She couldn't – must not – be in love with a man who had attempted to kill her half-sister three times, twice almost making Trish his unintentional victim instead. Now she understood his harsh "Go home" after the night of the fire. He meant go home before she got in his way and he accidentally hurt her!

And then an even more horrifying thought struck her. Marc, knowing that Edith's car would be parked at the village all day during the fiesta, must have tampered with the brakes early in the day. Then, attentive and charming, he had spent the afternoon and evening with Trish. He had kissed her into melting submission, suggested she leave with him. Perhaps he had been offering her more than a romantic interlude, Trish thought

195

now. Perhaps he had been offering her her life! He knew Edith's car would never survive the drive down the winding road, and he had offered Trish a chance to escape the death he had planned for Edith. But when she declined the offer, he was ruthlessly willing to sacrifice her if necessary to achieve his ends.

She remembered the resigned, almost regretful look on his face just before he left her that night. He was attracted to her, Trish was sure of that. But he would never let desire or attraction for a mere female stand in the way of his obsession to own the *cafetal*. He had cold-bloodedly decreed that if she must die to achieve his goal, then so be it. Nothing must interfere.

She felt drained, empty, numb. Without asking this time, Armando poured a drink for her and she gulped it down. He got up and went to stand by the window again, his stocky figure reflected in the dark frame. Somehow Trish was glad she could not see Marc's house.

"Do . . . do you think we should tell Edith all this?" Trish finally managed to say.

Armando shook his head. "Not yet, at any rate. Perhaps a little later, after she has had time to recover. I think the accident was enough shock for her just now."

Trish stared at her empty glass, her throat

still burning from the straight liquor. At this moment she wanted nothing so much as to pack her things and flee this tangled web of deception and danger. Perhaps, far, far away from Marc, his powerful male magnetism would lose its effect on her. Perhaps the ache of her love for him would fade. *It must!* she thought wildly. How could she love a man who had done the things he had, who ruthlessly sent her to what he expected to be certain death?

No, it wasn't love, she told herself determinedly. It was just infatuation, a physical reaction to his expert kisses and caresses. And the sooner she got away the better.

But Armando's next words, almost as if he knew what she was thinking, stopped her.

"Trish, you must not abandon Edith now," he said earnestly. "She needs you. She needs both of us. You must help me protect her from the clutches of this madman!"

Madman. Yes, Trish thought in some far-off corner of her mind. She had suspected Edith's father of being mad and murderous when he was only sick and confused. It was Marc, Marc, with his arrogant eyes and passionate kisses, who was the true madman, trapped by his obsession.

"But I don't know what I can do," she

197

protested doubtfully. "I haven't been much help so far."

"I don't know! Persuade Edith to marry me now, not wait for the big wedding," he said wildly. "What is a wedding anyway? A mere formality."

"But Edith has her heart set on it," Trish said. "Unless we tell her why the two of you shouldn't wait —"

"Then simply stay and watch over her," he begged. "You know the danger now. You are bright and clever and you will not accidentally fall into any more of Marcantonio de la Barca's vicious traps."

Except, she thought hollowly, she had already fallen into one of them, the most vicious trap of all. She was in love with him and he cared no more for her than some bit of rubbish, carelessly tossed away when its usefulness was gone.

But she must not let her need to escape her infatuation for the man drive her away and thus further endanger Edith's life, she thought determinedly. "I'm not leaving," she said firmly. "Edith is safe in the hospital. Perhaps we can persuade her to stay there as long as possible."

Armando reached over and squeezed her hand gratefully. "You have made me very happy. I thank you and I know Edith does

198

too . . . or will someday, when she knows."

But Trish's suggestion that Edith stay in the hospital as long as possible ran into an immediate snag. Edith did not want to stay in the hospital, saw no reason to stay there, and practically insisted she would not stay there.

Trish and Armando could not tell the doctor their reasons for wanting her to stay, of course, and his affable agreement that Edith could leave whenever she liked was hardly helpful. Trish persuaded Edith to stay a couple of extra days, but that was it. On the tenth day after the wreck, Armando and Trish brought her home in the Mercedes. Trish noted one thing when she was packing Edith's personal things to leave the hospital. There was a pack of cigarettes there, tucked far back in the corner of the nightstand. Probably few people knew she smoked, as Trish had not known. But Marc, after all the years of knowing and living next door to her, undoubtedly did know.

Edith was in excellent condition, considering her near collision with death. Her left arm was in a cast, and the scarf tied around her head didn't quite conceal the shaved area, but she had no problem walking or taking care of herself. On her very first night home she insisted on eating a regular meal in the dining room with Armando and

199

Trish. Afterward, she visited with her father for a while. Trish knew she must apologize for her suspicions about him, but that must wait until she could tell Edith why those suspicions had been abandoned. At this point, so far as Trish knew, Edith had no suspicion that her car wreck had been anything but a purely accidental brake failure.

It was too bad, Trish thought with a twinge of regret, that Robert Hepler felt about her the way he did. She would have liked to know this man, who had once been her mother's husband, who was her half-sister's father. Edith seemed to feel a great deal of affection for him, so surely Trish must have received a distorted, inaccurate impression of him that night in the hall. Trish knew she felt differently toward him because she no longer suspected him of trying to do her harm, that she felt vaguely guilty for even temporarily harboring those suspicions. If only she had listened to those stirrings of suspicion she felt about Marc, instead of labeling them preposterous and absurd!

That night, after seeing Edith safely in bed, Trish went to her own room and stared out the window for a long time without turning on the lights.

She could see dim lights at Marc's house, but she could not tell whether or not he was home. She still had not seen him since that morning at the hospital when he had so coldly held her away from him. Was he surprised that she had not also been involved in the car wreck? He hadn't really seemed so, but then his iron control would probably enable him to conceal anything he did not care to reveal. Or perhaps he didn't really care enough about her to register anything one way or the other; he had written her off when he turned and walked away from her the night of the fiesta.

And yet the way he had held her in his arms and kissed her that night. He hadn't seemed cold-blooded or uncaring. Far from it! She remembered the tremor of emotion at the corner of his mouth, a tremor that escaped even his rigid control. And even if his kisses were experienced and expert, they were certainly not lacking in passion.

If only she could talk to him! Perhaps there was some reasonable explanation that could answer all her doubts and suspicions. Perhaps behind that aloof, arrogant exterior Marc had actually been hurt by her rejection of him that night. Not that it was a real rejection of him, she thought, her hands trembling at the memory of that night as she moved the drape slightly for a better view. He didn't know that one more kiss, one more caress, and she would have abandoned all else and gone anywhere with him.

She got up and paced restlessly around the room. Yes, she must talk to him. It was unfair to condemn him without ever giving him the opportunity to defend himself.

Car lights arced across the window and Trish stopped short, realizing they had come from the direction of Marc's house. She darted to the window, saw the headlights stop in front of the house, and then blink out. It was too dark to see the vehicle behind the headlights, but she was sure it was Marc's car.

She hesitated a moment, wavering, wondering if she dared to do what she was considering. Yes, she decided. She had to do it, now, before she lost her nerve. If she thought too long about it, she knew common sense, or perhaps fear, would prevail. And the fact that he had returned home just now, when she felt a desperate need to talk to him, seemed somehow fortuitous, a sign that she should do it.

She slipped out of the shirtwaist dress she had worn to dinner and into sturdy jeans and a longsleeved blouse. As she left the room she carefully inspected the hall, not wanting to encounter Armando just then. She knew she could never give him a satisfactory explanation of why she was doing this. In fact, if she inspected her actions too closely, she might not have a logical explanation for herself. But then, was love ever logical?

The shortest route would have been to go by the swimming pool and out the courtyard gates, but there was too great a chance she would be seen. Instead she slipped out a side door and circled the house. There she hesitated again, undecided. Should she take the longer route by the road or the shorter but rougher route through the trees and brush? She glanced again at Marc's house. One more light had come on since his return. From the identical arrangement of rooms in the houses, she knew that it was a bedroom. Marc's bedroom?

That thought decided her. If he was preparing for bed, she must get to the house as quickly as possible, which meant taking the shorter route through the brush. This impetuous nighttime jaunt was already foolhardy enough without arousing Marc out of bed to talk to him!

She plunged into the dark tangle of underbrush, keeping her eyes on the bedroom light as a beacon to guide her. She determinedly kept her mind away from what might be beneath her feet, what her hands might encounter with each handhold on a hanging branch or vine. From Marc's stables she could hear the uneasy movement of horses' hooves, a nervous whinny now and then as the horses became aware of her awkward progress.

Finally she stumbled into the cleared area. She skirted the stable fences, careful to keep a good distance away from Demonio's paddock. She could hear him snorting in the darkness, contemptuous as always.

She was almost at the house when she saw the light in the bedroom go out. She paused, momentarily dismayed, but then proceeded determinedly. She had come this far; she was not going to turn back now.

She rounded the corner of the house and stepped into the shadows under the overhanging roof. She fumbled for a doorbell, could find none, and knocked instead. She waited, nervously phrasing and rephrasing what she wanted to say. No one came. She knocked again, louder and longer this time.

This time she was rewarded. Footsteps approached on the other side of the door.

Chapter Nine

A light flicked on over Trish's head, momentarily blinding her. She covered her eyes with her hands, and when she looked up, Marc was standing in the open doorway.

For a long moment they just stared at each other. Marc was wearing dark dress pants. Evidently he had started to undress and had flung a white shirt back on when he heard the knock on the door. The shirt hung open, his chest naked beneath it. The broad chest covered with fine dark hair tapered to a lean, tanned waist. Trish struggled against the feeling that always overwhelmed her in his powerful presence. There was something primitively suggestive about his naked skin bared beneath the expensive shirt.

Then Marc said coldly, "Yes?"

Trish's mouth felt dry, her tongue thick and awkward. "I ... I just wanted to talk to you. I mean, I must talk to you!" The statement sounded melodramatic with Trish in her old clothes, her hair awry from the struggle through the underbrush, the hour late, and Marc obviously preparing for bed.

"Couldn't it wait until a more suitable

time?" he suggested. Trish had the wild feeling he was going to pull out an appointment book and schedule some formal meeting date.

"No!" she cried. "I mean . . . things are happening. I'm frightened!"

Even in the shadowed doorway she could see his eyes narrow slightly. "Frightened of what?"

"May I come in?" Trish asked, feeling a little desperate. She shivered, half from nervous fear, half from the cold night air.

"Darling, what is it? Is something wrong?" The voice came from a figure that seemed to float toward them, the lush body momentarily outlined as the hall light glowed through the filmy peignoir. The woman moved toward Marc, and Trish knew who she was even before she reached the circle of his arm.

She was even more lovely than Trish remembered from her brief glimpse in the restaurant, her complexion like rich cream, her dark hair tumbling sensuously around her shoulders, the froth of a pale blue peignoir swirling around her voluptuous figure. Ramona de Cordoba. She had come from the direction of the bedroom light, the light that had gone out just before Trish arrived. She looked at Trish curiously, without recognition or antagonism – the same way one might look

206

at some unfortunate creature staggering on the streets, Trish thought wildly.

Trish's gaze jumped back to Marc. He had moved slightly and his face was in the full light now. There was the faint twist of a smile on his sensuous lips, and his dark eyes mocked her. She saw the deliberate tightening of his arm around the woman's shapely shoulders.

Trish took a stumbling step backward. "I – I'm sorry," she faltered. "I didn't know –"

She turned and fled, Ramona de Cordoba's musical voice drifting to her as she stumbled away. The words were in Spanish, totally incomprehensible to Trish at this stunned moment, but the tone, puzzled and a little amused, said enough.

Marc's words, spoken as if he said them with a shrug, were all too plain. "It was just that unpredictable American girl I was telling you about," he said carelessly to the beautiful woman at his side. "I'm sorry about the disturbance."

The words were said casually but spoken in English, for her benefit, Trish thought grimly. She plunged ahead into the darkness, hardly knowing where she was going, only wanting to get far away as quickly as possible, her heart and emotions in wild tumult.

When she finally paused for breath and

glanced back, the heavy door was shut, the light out.

What a fool she had been, telling herself Marc had perhaps been hurt by her rejection! She had half convinced herself that if only she could see and talk to him, everything could be explained satisfactorily. Now she knew the only explanation possible was the one she had fought against accepting.

Marc had realized that the only way he could buy the coffee plantation from Robert Hepler was if Edith were dead. He had cold-bloodedly decided to get rid of her, and if Trish got caught in the trap too, that was just too bad. He obviously had other willing arms with which to entertain and satisfy himself.

The thought of Marc making love to the lovely Ramona jolted through Trish with a fresh burst of pain. Irrational as it seemed, knowing what she did about him, her heart still ached at the thought of him with another woman. Even with the web of guilt tightening around him, the memory of his kisses and caresses made her heart pound. That made no sense, she thought wildly. She couldn't love a man so cruel and ruthless that he would kill to get what he wanted!

And yet she did love him. In spite of everything she had the sinking feeling that if he suddenly returned to the door and called to her, she would run to him.

She stood there for a moment longer, her chest rising and falling as she stared at the darkened house. Very well, she loved him, she admitted to herself. But she must not let that love blind her or get in the way of her duty to protect Edith. She must seal it off in some corner of her mind and heart, seal it off forever like an evil demon that must not be allowed to escape and drug her into some evil whirlpool of desire.

She walked on, trying not to think what was happening in the darkened house behind her.

She took the long way around by the road this time, past the coffee-processing plant and the neat office building. There was no need to hurry now. Edith was safe tonight. Marc was otherwise occupied. And there was little point in Trish hurrying home to her own bed. She knew it would be a long time before she slept tonight.

When she finally did sleep, it was with a kind of drugged stupor, and she awoke late the next morning, feeling sluggish and dispirited. Automatically she peered out the window in the direction of Marc's house. In the daylight, she could not pick out the bedroom window in which she had seen the light the night before. Unhappily she wondered if Ramona de Cordoba was even now looking back at her, her body still warm from Marc's caresses.

The thought made Trish feel sick inside and she determinedly jumped up, showered, and dressed. Today she was going to do something. She wasn't sure what, anything to keep her mind off Marc and Ramona – talk to Edith about the wedding, perhaps take her to see the seamstress and find out how the wedding dress was progressing. Perhaps she would get Edith to help her with her Spanish. That seemed an inspired idea. She couldn't possibly think about Marc when she was concentrating on mastering a foreign language.

That idea, she learned shortly, would have to be postponed. This was the doctor's day at the village and Edith, in spite of her broken arm and recent hospitalization, had determinedly gone over to the village to assist him.

That left Trish at loose ends. She restlessly tidied up her room, took a dip in the pool, and cut some flowers for the living room vases. While she was snipping some unfamiliar but flamboyantly red blooms, she heard a voice call from behind a bougainvillea-draped wall.

"Is that you, Edith?"

Trish froze in surprise. Robert Hepler! It had to be!

The voice came again, questioningly. "Edith?"

Trish glanced around in dismay, wondering what to do. In collecting the flowers, she had wandered around to the rear of the house, where she had not been before. She had seen the flower-draped wall from a distance but had vaguely assumed it was there to conceal a servants' entrance or utility activities. Now it appeared that assumption was in error, that the wall enclosed some sort of private patio Edith's father used.

Quickly Trish gathered up her armload of blooms. Her suspicions of Robert Hepler had vanished, but that had not changed his feelings about her nor the probability that seeing her would upset and disturb him. In her hurry she dropped the garden clippers and bent to retrieve them.

"You didn't answer. Is –"

Trish straightened up just as the tall, gaunt man rounded the end of the wall. They stared at each other for a long moment before Trish gathered her wits together and scrambled backward.

"Patricia?" he said tentatively.

Trish stopped at the unexpected and unfamiliar use of her full name and stared at him again. He was wearing khaki-colored walking shorts and a shortsleeved shirt that together revealed thin muscles and bony knees and elbows. But, as she had noted that day at the pool, there was really nothing frightening or peculiar looking about him. He was just a rather tired, old-looking man regarding her now with an unexpectedly hopeful look on his face.

"Yes. I . . . I'm Patricia Bellingham," Trish said uneasily.

If the last name of the man who had seduced his wife in any way affected him, he gave no indication of it.

"I'm Robert Hepler, Edith's father," he said. A rueful smile touched his gaunt face. "Don't be frightened of me, please. I've wanted to apologize for frightening you in the hallway that night. Edith had not told me you were coming and there in the dim light you looked so much like Edith's mother. It took me by surprise and it's no wonder my reaction frightened you. I'm very sorry."

He smiled again, a tentative, hopeful gesture that somehow reached out and touched Trish.

"I imagine I frightened you as much as you did me," she said, returning the smile tentatively. "Guests shouldn't wander around taking unexpected midnight swims."

"Would you come and have a glass of iced tea with me?" he suggested, motioning toward his small patio.

Trish hesitated, glancing uneasily toward the road. What would Edith think of this? But Robert Hepler did not appear to be upset or angry, so there seemed no reason to reject his cordial invitation. In fact Edith would probably be relieved when she learned she need not be apprehensive about her father and Trish encountering each other.

Robert Hepler led the way, slowly, and with some difficulty in walking, to the solid gate around the corner of the wall. He also had difficulty closing the latch behind them and Trish rushed to help.

"Useless hands," he muttered, grimacing as he looked at the gnarled fingers. He opened and closed his hands, a gesture Trish suddenly realized was something he did automatically, without thinking, to try to keep his hands flexible enough to use. He motioned her toward a small white patio table.

Trish took a seat, wondering where the private nurse was. A moment later the nurse rushed out, obviously agitated at finding Trish there.

"It's all right, Mrs. Spencer," Robert Hepler said calmly.

She clasped her hands. "But Edith said —"

"We're just having a glass of iced tea," Trish said, matching Robert Hepler's calm attitude. He gave her a conspiratorial smile and Trish smiled back.

Robert Hepler sighed as the woman went back inside, grumbling a bit to herself. "She means well. Edith does too. I'm sure that is why she's been so careful to keep us from meeting each other." He poured the tea and pushed sugar and lemon within Trish's reach. "But it wasn't really necessary."

"Edith will be glad to know that. I know I am," Trish said quickly. "I would never want my presence to upset you."

He twisted his glass and asked almost absentmindedly, "How is Carole Ann these days?"

"Oh . . . fine. I was raised mostly by my grandparents in Minnesota," Trish added, hoping to detour the conversation away from her mother. She rather liked the quiet man who had given her that unexpectedly conspiratorial smile, as if they were two children outwitting a stern adult, but she still wasn't sure of him."

"Yes, I remember your grandparents. Fine people," he murmured. "Do they still live on the little farm out of town?"

Trish nodded and went on to elaborate a bit on changes in the area, though he hardly seemed to be listening. Uneasily she realized Edith must have had good reasons for believing that seeing or talking to Trish would upset him.

"I'm afraid Edith still remembers my bitterness when her mother and I first separated. There were some rather unpleasant scenes," he said regretfully, as if sensing Trish's feelings. "But time changes our perspective and I am able to see things differently now. I hope time has softened Carole Ann's memories of me also."

Trish murmured something noncommittal. In truth her mother had hardly spoken of this man. Trish was curious about him but didn't want to pry. She sipped the iced tea, waiting to see if he would continue.

"I really can't blame her for what she did," he went on, looking off toward the mountain looming beyond them. "She had no idea when we married that I would immediately spirit her off to a remote Costa Rican banana plantation. She liked bright lights, happy times, and lots of social life. I gave her isolation, boredom, and an eccentric electric generator that wouldn't give any light about half the time," he added ruefully. "I was always tied up in my work. It's no wonder she fell for the first attractive man who appeared and paid her some real attention."

215

Trish knew vaguely that her parents had met while her father was in Costa Rica with the import firm in which he had eventually become an important executive, but she had never known any of the details. She had been in her teens, in fact, before she realized that falling in love with Roger Bellingham was what had broken up her mother's marriage to Robert Hepler. She was glad now that time had obviously healed that painful wound in Robert Hepler, but she would just as soon talk about something else. Robert Hepler was beginning to look almost morose as he stared at the icy liquid in his glass.

"Costa Rica is certainly a lovely place," Trish said suddenly, too brightly. Almost grasping at straws, she added, "Edith told me once you used to hunt for Indian artifacts on the other side of the mountain."

"Yes, near the old lava tubes. I never found anything but it's an interesting area. I always thought it might have been an old burial site. Peculiar, the way the lava hardened on the outside and then flowed on through, leaving those big, empty tubes and caverns. I explored some of them, but it is an eerie place."

He lapsed into silence as if his mind were really elsewhere. Trish jumped up suddenly, making an almost exaggerated gesture of looking at her watch.

"I didn't realize it was getting so late! And I must get these flowers in water before they wilt." She scooped up the armload of flowers she had set beside her chair. "I've really enjoyed talking to you, Mr. Hepler."

"Mr. Hepler," he mused. "That sounds so formal."

"Yes, I suppose it does," she said, suddenly a little uneasy at the odd way he was looking at her. She managed a bright smile. "And do call me Trish. No one calls me by my full name."

"Trish," he murmured. He smiled. "A bit impudent sounding. Yes, that suits you."

"Do you go by Robert?" she asked. "Or Bob?"

"Robert," he said absentmindedly. "Once upon a time . . . a long, long time ago, your mother used to call me Robbie. But –" He broke off, swallowing convulsively. "It would please me very much if just once I could hear you call me Father. Or maybe . . . maybe even Dad."

Trish stared at him, aghast. Everything had seemed so normal about him up to now, just a pleasant, reminiscing sort of conversation between two people sipping iced tea together on a sunny day. But was that normalcy all just a facade? What confused thoughts could

217

possibly make him want her to call him Father? But there was such a pleading, almost desperate look on his gaunt face tht she didn't want to argue. She moved as unobtrusively as possible toward the gate.

"Very well, F-Father," she managed to say. She held the armload of flowers between them almost like a shield.

He smiled ruefully. "I've frightened you again, haven't I? I'm sorry. I know I must sound mad to you. I shouldn't have said anything. I promised I never would."

Once again he was just an old and tired man automatically flexing his hands to keep them from becoming completely bent and stiff and useless. "I'm sorry," he repeated gently.

"No, please, I don't understand." Trish took a step toward him. The sunny day suddenly seemed strange and unreal around her, the ground insubstantial beneath her as she wavered on the edge of a never even suspected discovery. "Who did you promise? What did you promise?"

"Your mother," he said simply. "That I would never tell anyone I was your real father."

The blooms dropped nervelessly from Trish's arms. She sank weakly into the wooden chair, stunned by the relevation and yet never for a moment doubting it.

The quiet, simple statement had the ring of utter truth. She moistened dry lips. "I – I don't understand."

"During the worst of the hot, humid season on the banana plantation my wife would go into San José for a few weeks each year. One year she met Roger Bellingham. They fell in love. She came back to the plantation and told me." He said it all matter-of-factly, without emotion, then sighed. "I made a terrible scene. I threatened, pleaded, everything. Finally she said she would forget Bellingham and stay. We made up, after a fashion, but she was miserably unhappy. Then, a couple of months later, Bellingham showed up at the plantation, saying he had come to take her away. This time Carole Ann said she was going, that I could not stop her, and she was taking our daughter, Edith, with her."

He paused, and took a sip from the glass that now held only melted ice water. Trish could see his hand trembling on the glass.

"By then I knew I had lost my . . . my wife. But I vowed she would never have Edith. And by then I had a weapon to use against her, because she was pregnant again. With you."

Trish caught her breath, and found herself gripping the table so tightly her hand felt numb.

"Bellingham didn't know. Looking back,

I doubt now that it would have made any difference to him if he had known. But at the time I thought it would matter and Carole Ann was desperately afraid it would affect his feelings for her. I warned her that if she took Edith away, I would make sure Bellingham knew the truth. But if she would leave Edith, she could go and good riddance. She could try to deceive Bellingham any way she wanted. We struck a sort of bargain: If she would leave Edith with me and never interfere with her in any way, I would do the same with the unborn child she was carrying and never reveal I was the real father." He stopped, his face troubled. "And now I have broken that vow."

Trish reached over and squeezed his bony hand reassuringly. "I think after all these years that my mother would perhaps not object too much. And I . . . I am very grateful that I know the truth."

Roger Bellingham already knew the truth, she added to herself. Perhaps Carole Ann had concealed the fact of her pregnancy for a short while, until there was time to let him think the coming child was his. Perhaps she even carried the deception so far as to say the baby arrived abnormally early. But Roger Bellingham, though he might have pretended to accept the deception, knew who

220

the baby's real father was. Trish had no doubt about that.

The child. The baby. Trish realized she was thinking as if this had happened to someone else. This child was she! And it explained so many things.

It explained why she had been raised by her grandparents, staying with them even when her parents were not traveling, something that had puzzled and sometimes even hurt her. It explained why Roger Bellingham, although always treating Trish with kindness and generosity, had never been very close or affectionate to her. It explained too, Trish thought suddenly, her mother's seeming indifference to Edith all these years. That had been a part of the bargain.

"Does Edith know?" Trish asked suddenly.

Robert Hepler shook his head. "I've kept it a secret all this time. Only my lawyer knows. I've wanted to tell Edith, but . . ." He lifted his hands helplessly.

"Would you mind very much if I told her?" Trish asked. "I think it would make her feel better to know why our mother has always been so . . . indifferent to her."

Robert Hepler looked troubled again. "I should not have told you. I never intended to. Your mother will never forgive me if she finds out. But seeing you, seeing the fear in your eyes when you looked at me . . ."

"I'm glad you told me," Trish said sincerely. She couldn't explain all the strange feelings that were suddenly coursing through her. "I'm just glad. And I think Edith would be glad to know too."

Robert Hepler finally nodded and Trish sat there trying to take it all in. It didn't make her feel any different toward the man she had always thought of as her father, Roger Bellingham, she realized slowly. In fact she felt she could somehow better accept him for what he was, a man who had accepted another man's child and done the best he could for her. Too often she had thought his lack of demonstrativeness toward her had resulted from a lack in her, that if only she were smarter or prettier or more talented he would have been more loving. Somehow it was easier knowing, even at this late date, that his feelings had nothing to do with her personal attributes. Edith, she thought suddenly, might feel that way too. Had she perhaps felt that if she were prettier or smarter that her mother would have loved her enough to stay?

Oh, the burdens and guilts we take on ourselves as children, Trish thought ruefully. She suddenly realized Robert Hepler was looking at her anxiously. It was difficult to think of him as her father, but not impossible. Impulsively she reached over and hugged him, and a smile of pure pleasure lit his gaunt face.

Suddenly there were so many things she wanted to ask him. Half of her very being was a complete unknown to her. But she could see that telling her all this, almost reliving it, had tired and weakened his already frail body.

"We'll talk again," she promised. "But now I think you should get some rest."

He nodded and she helped him lie down on a padded lounge chair. He touched her hand in a small gesture of gratitude.

"You'll tell Edith?"

She nodded and patted his arm reassuringly. "There is no need for anyone else to know, if you think it would be better that way." She paused, remembering something, though she never knew later just why she chose to ask the question. "But you mentioned that someone else did know? A lawyer?"

"Yes. Hans Schwarz. He's handled the plantation legal matters for years."

Hans Schwarz. She might not have remembered the name if it had not seemed so incongruous among the mostly Spanish-sounding names she had encountered in this country. Now it flashed across her mind like a brilliant neon sign. Hans Schwarz – the very

223

same lawyer Marc had gone to see in San José.

It didn't necessarily mean anything, she told herself. It was probably logical that the same lawyer took care of business matters for both *cafetales*, since they were, though perhaps unwillingly, partners of a sort. And yet . . . Something nibbled at the edge of her mind, something not quite formed into a thought, and yet somehow already filling her with a vague apprehension. She realized Robert Hepler was speaking to her again.

". . . could have dinner together some evening, if you don't mind my rather clumsy tendency to spill and drop things."

"We'll do that," Trish said quickly, reassuringly. "You get some rest now."

"Trish?"

"Yes?"

"I - I'm very proud of you. It makes me very happy to have both my daughters here."

Trish gave him another hug and gathered up the blooms she had dropped. She waved and smiled as she went out the gate. But once on the other side, the thought that had nibbled at the edge of her mind exploded into a full-blown realization.

Marc knew! Somehow through his association with the same lawyer Robert Hepler used, Marc had managed to find out she was really the daughter of Edith's father.

When had he found out? Had he known all along? Or was it a recent discovery, perhaps made the very day he and Trish had gone to San José? What did it all mean?

Trish's thoughts churned chaotically. If Marc knew she was a true daughter of the owner of the *cafetal* he coveted, did he also think she possessed some claim to the property just as Edith did? Did he think that even if he got rid of Edith, Trish might still stand in his way? She couldn't, of course. Her birth certificate showed Roger Bellingham as her father. She could never make any valid legal claim to the property. But Marcantonio de la Barca was a determined and thorough man. If he thought there was a chance, any chance at all, that Trish might stand in his way, he would be only too willing to get rid of her along with Edith.

The car "accident" had offered the perfect opportunity to kill them both, she thought with a shudder. With both his daughters dead, sick and grieving Robert Hepler would be only too glad to get rid of the coffee plantation and sell it to Marc. How disappointed Marc must have been to hurry to the hospital the morning after the car wreck and find Trish there, whole and healthy, and Edith only injured. No wonder he had been so cold and aloof!

225

Trish had already accepted the fact that Marc was ruthlessly willing to let her die as a sort of coincidental by-product of his getting rid of Edith, but now she had to face the fact that he might actually have deliberately planned her death also – planned it at the very moment he was kissing and caressing her at the fiesta!

But he had offered her a way of escape, she thought with a sudden surge of hope. He had tried to get her to leave the fiesta with him. Or had he? Moment by moment her mind went back over the sweet pain of those minutes in the dark as she struggled to pinpoint each word he had spoken, each nuance of meaning.

And then she had to stifle an almost hysterical laugh at her own naiveté. Marc had made some whispered comment about going to his car; she had interpreted this as a suggestion that she leave with him. But what was he really suggesting? A few moments of crude, meaningless passion in his car? And she had thought him so sophisticated, so charming. Was there ever anyone so blind as a woman in love? The full horror of his ruthlessness settled around her like an icy cloud; the realization that he could try to seduce her and then cold-bloodedly send her to her death. And she had no doubt but that if his expert kisses and caresses had succeeded, he would still have sent her to her death. He was willing to mix business and pleasure when convenient, but he never forgot that business, the business of possessing the *cafetal*, came first. And she had naively gone to him wanting to talk! How he must have laughed at her.

Trish felt something sticky on her arms and glanced down, realizing in dismay that in her mental turmoil she had carelessly crushed and ruined the flamboyant red blooms. It seemed symbolic of the careless way Marc had been willing to destroy her. The red stain of the flowers might have been her own blood. . . .

She walked to the edge of the clearing and dropped the limp blooms into the tangled underbrush. It seemed a regrettable waste. A short time ago they had been glowing and alive on the shrubs; now they were dead and wasted. She looked at them with remorseful guilt, wondering wildly if Marc would feel even the faintest twinge of regret when he sent her to her death.

Now she was becoming melodramatic and morbid, she told herself unsteadily. She had to get hold of herself, straighten out her thoughts and emotions. But too much had assaulted her mind this day – the startling revelation of her true heredity, and the fresh

227

damnation of the man with whom she had recklessly, precipitously fallen in love.

Chapter Ten

Edith looked stunned when Trish finished telling everything their father had related to her. They were sitting in Edith's bedroom, which looked out on the brilliant courtyard.

"It makes me happy to know we're really sisters," Trish added. "I hope you're pleased too."

"Oh, I am!" Edith agreed quickly, her gaze jerking back from the light dancing off the pool.

"But there is one thing. Your father . . . our father . . . seemed worried that he had done something wrong in telling me because of that old promise he made to our mother. I tried to reassure him, but maybe if you could say something too?" Trish suggested.

"Yes, I'll do that." Edith nodded.

Trish considered warning her about the dangers to both of them from Marc, but Edith seemed so stunned by this first piece of information that Trish decided against saying anything more just then. Edith was absentmindedly massaging the fingers protruding from the cast on her left arm.

"Will you tell Armando?" Trish asked.

"I don't know. Yes, I suppose so," Edith said. She sounded distracted, more shocked than Trish had been by the revelation.

Trish squeezed her arm. "Why don't you lie down and take a nap before dinner? You look exhausted. You really shouldn't be up and running around, you know."

Edith nodded. "Yes, I'll do that." She hesitated. "Did Father say anything more?"

"About what?"

"Oh, I don't know. Mother, us . . ."

"Just that he wasn't bitter against her anymore. I hope you can feel that way too," Trish added impulsively. "It must have been very difficult for you all these years when she acted so indifferent toward you. But now you know the reason why."

"Yes," Edith murmured. "Now I know."

"It wasn't really by choice," Trish added.

"Wasn't it?" Edith murmured, but she sounded more tired than bitter.

Trish went to her own room then. She had to admit she was a little disappointed that Edith hadn't seemed more excited about the news, but she reflected that the quiet reaction was typical of Edith's reserved, unassuming character. By dinnertime Edith did seem more enthusiastic and approving, almost vivacious perhaps, Trish realized, because Edith had told Armando the news and he approved, and so that made everything all right.

Armando, in fact, seemed quite delighted. He proposed a toast with the dinner wine, showered both Trish and Edith with extravagant compliments, insisted on taking a snapshot of them together, and generally turned the evening into a festive occasion of celebration. He made no mention of the dangers from Marc and Trish decided to ignore them for the moment too. The happy camaraderie among the three of them was too good to spoil this evening.

The next morning, however, when Edith excused herself after breakfast to go see her father, Trish brought up the subject to Armando in low tones, ever mindful that whatever they said might find its way to Marc. She explained her new suspicion that Marc might mistakenly believe she had some claim on the *cafetal* and want to get rid of her as well as Edith. Armando was considering the matter thoughtfully when Edith unexpectedly rushed into the dining room.

"Father is gone!" she cried.

Armando looked up. "Gone? Gone where?" he asked, looking mildly puzzled. "Perhaps he's taking a walk with the nurse."

Edith shook her head wildly. "No! He left a note. And the nurse is practically in a stupor. He must have tricked her into taking some of his sleeping pills!"

Armando took the note from Edith and spread it on the table. The writing was plain enough, but the message was rambling and disjointed. It went on about how he should never have revealed the truth to Trish, that he had made a sacred promise to her mother not to, that he could no longer live with this burden of guilt on his heart.

"What does he mean?" Edith cried. "Why has he done this?"

"He isn't reasoning logically anymore," Armando said grimly. "His mind has become completely unbalanced. We must find him before he does something terrible."

"But he seemed so normal yesterday," Trish protested.

"Is it normal to say you're going to some ancestral place to die?" Armando asked, pointing to the last cryptic sentence.

"What does it mean?" Edith repeated. "Where did he go?"

"To the lava tubes!" Trish gasped. "He said something only yesterday about their being a possible burial site."

"We have no time to waste then," Armando said grimly. "We have no idea when he left

231

here. He could be hours ahead of us."

"But he couldn't walk there, could he?" Trish asked. "It's a long distance and he could barely get around yesterday."

Edith paused uncertainly and looked at Armando. He nodded.

"That's true. Perhaps we are in luck then. If we leave right now, perhaps we can catch him before he reaches the tunnels and carries out whatever he has in mind."

Armando issued crisp instructions about wearing sturdy shoes and taking jackets in case they had to search the tunnels. He was instructing a servant to bring flashlights when Trish hurried off to change her clothes. Only moments later the three of them were in the pickup, churning up the slope through the coffee trees.

Beyond the cultivated area the road was no more than two rough ruts overgrown from disuse. Low branches drooped overhead and Trish automatically dodged as a branch slapped the windshield now and then. This was all her fault, she thought remorsefully. She should have turned and run the moment she saw Robert Hepler. Edith had been right in keeping them apart. She knew any contact with Trish would upset him. Edith might have been mistaken about the reason he would be disturbed, but the outcome was the same. Only worse, Trish thought unhappily, because even Edith had never suspected something like this might happen. What did the man intend to do? Had he taken a weapon? Or did he intend to crawl off into some hidden niche and wait for death?

The pickup, roaring over the rough terrain, was too noisy for conversation. Using shouts and motions, Armando told Edith to watch for her father on one side of the vehicle. Trish on the other. It took all his attention to keep the pickup upright and moving ahead. Trish watched so intently, her eyes hurt, knowing Robert Hepler – somehow she still couldn't think of him freely as her father – might hide in the brush when he heard them coming.

Almost abruptly the pickup broke out of the trees and brush and onto the barren lava area. Up close it looked even more like a congealed mass of monstrous, prehistoric snakes, with here and there some nightmare shape rising above the strange, twisting tubes.

The road descended along the edge of the deep, hardened mass, and it wasn't difficult to imagine some fresh tide of lava flowing over that edge and engulfing them. Firmly Trish jerked her mind away from such wild imaginings and concentrated on looking for Robert Hepler. But her senses were jolted again when Armando stopped the pickup in front of a dark, cavelike hole. Just looking at it Trish felt a crawling sense of claustrophobia.

"This is the main entrance," Armando said. "Several tubes lead off it. We'll separate and each search a tunnel. Don't give up until you can go no farther. Some hidden, hard-to-reach spot may be just what he is looking for."

"But wouldn't it be better if we stayed together?" Trish asked doubtfully. "I mean . . . could he be dangerous?"

Armando handed her a flashlight. "Only to himself. We'll take too long if we stay together and we may not have much time. Don't forget your jackets," he instructed. "It's cold in there."

Edith was already slipping her arms into a heavy sweater. Slowly, feeling guilty at her reluctance to enter the dark hole, Trish put on her jacket and zipped it up. Then Armando led the way.

The change in temperature was apparent only a few feet inside the tunnel. The air smelled damp, musty, and unused, and Trish was nervously conscious of the deep, hardened river of lava above them. She clutched her flashlight, trying to calm her panicky feeling of claustrophobia. She turned to look back at the circle of sunlight behind them. It took all her willpower not to flee to its bright safety. Already she felt the strange eeriness Robert

Hepler had mentioned.

"Do you really think he came here?" she asked doubtfully. Her voice sounded hollow.

"I don't think there's any doubt of it, especially after he mentioned the place to you only yesterday," Armando said.

Armando's flashlight, more powerful than the other two, lit up the rough walls of the tunnel. The tunnel was larger than Trish had realized at first, the ceiling a good five or six feet above her head, but the knowledge did nothing to loosen that tight feeling of claustrophobia. Farther back the tunnel separated into several smaller tubes. Trish stared at them in dismay as Armando's flashlight paused momentarily on each dark, forbidding hole. Without waiting for instructions from Armando, Edith started determinedly toward the center tube. Armando looked inquiringly at Trish.

"That one, I guess," Trish said uneasily, pointing to an opening taking off at an angle to the right.

"Don't be afraid," Armando said, patting her arm reassuringly. "Just remember, he is your father and he needs your help. Be thorough. He may try to hide."

Trish nodded and switched on her flashlight, shivering slightly as she stepped alone into the hollow tube that was barely high enough to clear her head. She stopped and nervously played the beam over the walls. When she turned and looked back, Armando's light had already disappeared into one of the other tunnels. The bright circle of outdoor light was gone too, cut off by the angle of the lava tube.

Trish advanced slowly, the flashlight held in front of her as if its beam was some sort of magical protection. This tunnel led away from the others, deep under the mountain. It weighed down on her, made her chest feel tight and heavy. Her hand grew numb from gripping the flashlight, and the cold penetrated her fingers.

The utter silence was unearthly, the only sound her own ragged breathing and the reluctant shuffle of her feet. A small rustle behind her made her whirl in near terror. Shakily she realized it was only a bit of the volcanic rubble dislodged by her foot, and she leaned weakly against the rough wall. By now the tube was smaller, and she had to walk slightly bent over. She knew she would soon be down on her hands and knees and she didn't know if she could stand that or not. Already her stomach was tight and nervous as the tube closed in around her. The tunnel was so narrow that she had to keep her arms tucked close to her sides, and the ceiling close above her seemed to bear down on her like some immense weight.

Then she heard something. A rustle? A tapping? Cautiously she moved forward, wincing once as a strand of hair caught on the low ceiling overhead. The sound was regular, rhythmic. She rounded a bend in the tunnel and then saw what she had heard, water seeping through the top of the tunnel and dripping into the porous rock below. She wanted to feel relief but there was something eerie about the steady, impersonal dripping. She had the wild feeling that if she were there very long it could send her into screaming hysteria. Her earlier apprehension that Robert Hepler might be dangerous had been lost in fear of the strange tunnel itself. It was like a trap, she thought shakily. A trap yawning open, waiting, only to close silently behind any intruder.

Then she noticed something else. The water had brought with it over the years a layer of fine sand or dirt that covered the tunnel floor for some fifteen or twenty feet ahead. Tentatively Trish stepped onto the damp material. Her foot left a definite, unmistakable imprint. She probed the wide expanse of damp sand quickly with her flashlight beam. It was completely untouched, no trace of any footprint. Robert Hepler could not have crossed it without leaving footprints and so obviously he had not come this way. Relief surged over Trish. There was no need to go farther. She could turn back now.

She did so, her eager footsteps taking her back considerably faster than she had come. She was surprised when she reached the junction of the small tube with the main tunnel so quickly. It seemed as if she had gone much farther into the bowels of the earth. Now the large entrance tunnel looked almost spacious and the tight feeling in her chest relaxed as if an iron band had been released. It was lighter here and she switched off the flashlight and stuck it in her jacket pocket. She breathed deeply, then hurried forward, anxious to get out in the sunlight. Somehow she was convinced Robert Hepler was not in this strange place and they would be better to recruit helpers and search the area closer to the house.

She stopped short, blinking at the glare of light even though the tunnel entrance was still some distance away. Two figures were silouetted against the light, one standing, one bent over. Trish hesitated, puzzled, but then the bent figure straightened and she recognized Armando's stocky but well-built figure. The other one was Edith, the awkward cast and some oddly shaped object she was holding momentarily making her mature figure unrecognizable.

"Did you find him?" Trish called.

Armando jerked as if surprised to hear a voice. "No, no we didn't," he said slowly. His voice had an oddly unconcerned tone. He sounded almost amused as he added, "But then I didn't think we would."

"You didn't?" Trish asked, bewildered. She started forward.

"That's far enough," Armando said sharply.

Trish stopped, even more bewildered. "What? Is something wrong?"

"Not that I know of," Armando answered pleasantly.

He bent over again, doing something with some object on the tunnel floor, but with the light behind them Trish couldn't tell what it was. A wave of apprehension swept over her.

"Tell me what is going on," she demanded. "Where is Robert Hepler?"

"I imagine he's enjoying the sun on his patio with his nurse," Armando said calmly. "Wasn't that where he was when you left him, Edith?"

Edith said nothing, but with a sick feeling Trish realized no comment was necessary. Something was wrong, terribly, frighteningly wrong. Trish did not know what it was but she did not intend to stay in this eerie tunnel and play mysterious word games with Armando. She marched forward determinedly.

"Stop right there." It was Edith's voice now, shaky but also determined. "Don't come any closer."

Trish hesitated but did not stop. Armando did not seem to be paying any attention to her now. He was off to the side of the tunnel with what looked like a roll of wire in his hand.

"I mean it!" Edith cried. "Stop!"

"No," Trish said, still walking forward. "I don't understand any of this, but we can talk about it out in the daylight."

Trish heard something then, a metallic click, and at the same moment, Edith moved. She was still in silhouette with the light behind her, her face invisible, but there was no mistaking the object in her arms. A rifle.

"Edith, this is insane!" Trish gasped. "What are you doing?"

The answer came from Armando. "Just a few fireworks." He had the flashlight turned on now, the beam pointed down toward the objects he was working with. "Only this time they'll be a bit more powerful. But the show will take a few minutes to prepare. You came back sooner than we expected."

The glow of the flashlight reflected on his face, turning the handsome features into an unearthly devil mask. Trish gasped. It was if the veneer of smooth sophistication had been stripped away, leaving only the hidden, raw evil of his character. Trish's mind reeled, unable to comprehend any of this, knowing only that her life was in danger.

"Edith?" she appealed tentatively.

"Why didn't you die in the fire the first night the way you were supposed to!" Edith cried, her voice anguished. "It would have been so much easier that way!"

"The fire. You set the fire?" Trish gasped.

Armando spoke. "I put the burning cigarette in your room, though I had to watch and wait until you finished your foolish midnight swim first. The cigarette was supposed to catch the curtains. Instead it fell on the mattress and smoldered there." He sounded disgusted. "And then I had to unlock the door when you screamed loud enough to wake the dead."

Trish's mind spun dizzily, hardly able to believe what he was saying. "And the accident with the horse?" Trish asked, her voice rising in panic. "You fired the shots. There was no injured relative!"

"How clever of you to figure that out," Armando complimented sarcastically. "As a matter of fact I purchased the horse because he was terrified of gunshots. It seemed a trait

241

that might prove useful."

Trish's mind wouldn't seem to function, couldn't seem to make sense out of all this. All she could think was that she had blamed Marc for everything. Marc! And all the time it was Armando who was the consummate actor, Armando with his logical, believable explanations about how and why Marc was trying to commit murder!

"Edith, I can't believe this is happening," Trish gasped. "We're sisters!"

"Of course we're sisters," Edith said contemptuously. Her voice was no longer shaky. Now it was as cold and hard as Armando's. "Do you think, from the time I was old enough to think about such things, that I couldn't count on my fingers and realize there was a very good chance we were full sisters?"

"But you seemed so stunned when I told you —"

"Stunned that now you knew the truth too," Edith said coldly. "It didn't seem important when I first suspected it long ago. It didn't matter. Not until I found the will."

"What will?" Trish asked.

"My father's will, of course. Leaving half of his estate to you!"

Trish felt dizzy. Armando raised his flashlight suddenly and the beam hit Trish

242

full in the face. She threw up her arm to shield her eyes. Then the beam moved impersonally on by her as Armando continued with what he was doing.

"You planned it all, didn't you?" Trish asked tremulously. "From the very beginning. That's why you invited me down here. Not to be with you at your wedding but to get rid of me so the *cafetal* would be all yours when your father died."

Edith moved, resting the rifle lightly against her hip. Trish knew her sister would have no hesitation about using the gun. Trish now realized what had happened. The fact that they were sisters probably hadn't seemed important to Edith, not until Armando came along and the will was discovered. How had Armando reacted when he learned Edith would not inherit the entire *cafetal* when her father died, that she would have to share it with some bothersome American sister? Then their relationship had become important, deadly important. Because if Edith lost half the plantation, she also lost Armando. And Edith, it was obvious, would do anything to keep from losing Armando.

The silence hung between them, interrupted only by a few small rustlings from where Armando worked, ignoring them.

"I – I'm really sorry it has to be this way,"

Edith said suddenly. She sounded almost regretful as she added, "It sounded so simple when we planned it before you arrived. But then I found I really rather liked you."

"Liked me!" Trish's voice sounded shrill to her own ears, verging on wild hysteria. "You can hold a gun on me and say you liked me? You're going to kill me and you say you liked me?"

The words seemed to echo around them and the two women stared at each other. Kill me ... kill me ... kill me. Trish felt dazed as with her own words the full force of terror hit her. They were going to kill her. Whatever Armando was working on was the instrument of death.

"For God's sake, don't make this any more difficult than it already is!" Edith cried suddenly. "I was so sure it was over when Armando came back to the car and said you were lying dead at the top of the mountain. And then we got back to the house and there you were ... alive! And I realized we had to do it all over again."

Trish remembered that day of her "accident" with the horse, remembered how stunned Edith had seemed. Trish had put all the wrong interpretation on that. She had put all the wrong interpretation on Marc's actions too, she thought with bitter anguish.

Edith went on, almost as if she were talking to herself now. "I was so afraid you'd leave, and yet I hated the thought of having to try again. You were so nice to me."

Edith's voice drifted off vaguely, as if her determination to carry this through had weakened. Trish tried to press her slight advantage.

"Edith, we're sisters. Do you think you can live with yourself if you do this thing? And what about your father?" she added with sudden inspiration. "You love him. I know you do. Will you hurt him more by destroying me?"

"She's trying to play on your emotions now," Armando warned. "Watch out."

Edith seemed to get hold of herself. The rifle, which had momentarily sagged in her arms, lifted again. Trish could see the silhouette of the butt cradled under Edith's right arm, the barrel supported by her fingers protruding from the cast.

"Neither my father nor I need you," Edith said coldly. "We got along just fine without you all these years. You have no right to any part of the plantation."

"You really did it all, didn't you?" Trish said, still incredulous in spite of what was happening in front of her very eyes. "The fire . . . the accident with the horse . . .

the car wreck. That was meant for me too, I suppose." Trish's voice rose hysterically. "What went wrong there? Did you make a mistake and get caught in the trap you had set for me?"

"That's enough," Armando said harshly. "There is no need for all this chatter. Everything is ready."

But Trish wouldn't be silenced as fresh truths dawned on her. "You were never worried about my meeting your father, our father, because it might upset him, were you? You were willing to let me think he was mentally deranged to keep me from talking to him. You were afraid if I did talk to him and learned the truth I'd suspect you were out to get rid of me!"

"But you weren't that clever, were you?" Armando remarked, sounding evilly amused. "You went running to Edith to tell her the good news about your being sisters. When Edith's father 'disappeared,' you even conveniently suggested where he might have gone and saved us the trouble of having to convince you to come here."

With a sense of desolation, Trish realized that was exactly what she had done. And she had swallowed Armando's clever, twisted accusations against Marc all the way. Oh, if only she had told Marc everything. If only she

246

had ignored her jealous heart when she found him with another woman! What did any of that matter now?

Armando almost seemed to read her mind. He laughed an ugly, humorless sound. "I was afraid you'd get to Marcantonio de la Barca and tell him you and Edith were sisters. He'd have known what was going on then." Armando's voice hardened and he spit out an epithet about Marc. "Always so damn clever and suspicious, always snooping around."

"But you won't get away with this!" Trish cried. "Marc . . . Marc cares for me! I know he does. He'll search for me!"

"Yes, Marc is in love with you. You should have had more faith in him," Armando said dispassionately. "But it does not matter now."

"He'll ask questions!"

"Marc and everyone else will be told you suddenly decided to return to the States. Marc will have no difficulty finding consolation in other feminine arms, as I'm sure you realize."

He said it with the deliberate intent of hurting her, Trish knew. He was enjoying her pain. Physical torment wasn't enough for him; he had to wound her very soul too.

"But my father might not believe that story," Edith said suddenly, sounding worried. "He'll think it peculiar that Trish went away without saying good-bye."

Armando cursed again. "I told you you should have sent him away a long time ago! He's just a talkative old fool. But you were sentimental, you had to keep him around. We wouldn't have had to rush things if he hadn't told Trish everything."

Even seen in silhouette Trish could distinguish the slight drawing back that marked Edith's shock at Armando's outburst. Trish knew it was her last chance to work on Edith's sympathy.

"Think about all this!" Trish said. "If Armando wants the coffee plantation so desperately that he's willing to kill me for it, don't you think that someday he may decide you are in the way too? Do you want a man who loves you only if you own a *cafetal* . . . a man who won't marry you if you don't stand to inherit it free and clear? And what happens if that inheritance takes too long? What comes next? Killing your father?"

Edith caught her breath so sharply that even Trish could hear it. With sudden intuition Trish knew this was not a totally new thought to Edith, that the very same suspicion had occurred to her in spite of her love for Armando. The gun wavered and sagged.

But then Armando walked over and put his arm around Edith's shoulders and Trish knew she had lost. She didn't need to see his triumphant smile to know it was there. Edith had momentarily wavered, but her passion for Armando was stronger than anything else.

"I do not care to listen to your lies," she said firmly. Her head turned to look up at Armando. "I love Armando. He loves me."

"Edith, I don't want any part of the *cafetal*. I don't want anything!" Trish cried desperately. "Tear up the will. Why didn't you tear it up to begin with?"

"Because it is only a copy, not the original," Armando said. His voice sounded incongruously kind, as if he were explaining something to a simpleminded child. "It would do no good to tear up a copy."

"But I know where the original must be!" Trish said with sudden inspiration. "A lawyer in San José has it. His name is Hans Schwarz."

Edith had turned to look at Trish and now she glanced up at Armando again. Trish could tell she was wavering a little.

"There's no need to kill me," Trish said wildly. "Just get the will, tear it –"

"No!" Armando interjected harshly. "This is the way it must be done."

His arm dropped from Edith's shoulders

and he strode over to where he had been working. Edith took an oddly imploring step toward Trish.

"I'm sorry," she almost whispered. "I really am."

Those were the last words Trish heard before the tunnel exploded in front of her in a blinding, deafening blast. The last thing she saw were the figures of Edith and Armando silhouetted against the circle of light and freedom. And then an avalanche of exploding rock blotted out everything.

Chapter Eleven

The image burned in Trish's mind, a stark etching of black and white – the silhouetted figures, the blazing circle of light that was the tunnel entrance, the rain of rock caught motionless in space. She blinked, but the scene didn't change, the rock didn't fall, the figures with outflung arms didn't move.

Trish became vaguely conscious that something was pressing against her back, that her head hurt. There was a peculiar taste in her mouth and a choking, dusty smell in the air. She reached up, trembling, to touch her lips. They were wet and she knew the strange taste in her mouth was blood. But when she tried to look at her hand, all she could see was that black-and-white scene, and when she tried to look around, it was everywhere, on all sides of her, burned into her mind and senses.

Unsteadily she struggled to her feet, blinking, trying to erase the image that wouldn't go away. Something clattered to the ground as she stood up. The flashlight. She groped for it and fumbled for the switch.

The beam lit up the tunnel and the silhouetted figures in her mind vanished, only to be replaced by a nightmare scene of reality and destruction. Huge chunks of shattered lava filled the tunnel. A fine dust hung in the air and Trish coughed, her nose and throat thick with it.

It took a moment before full comprehension hit her, and then she reeled under the impact of it. She was sealed inside the lava tubes, trapped behind an avalanche of rock under the mountain with no way of escape. No escape!

No, that couldn't be! Frantically she clambered over the jumbled rock, clawing and fighting, searching for some opening. She flung smaller rocks aside, sent a larger one crashing headlong to the tunnel floor. She had to get out . . . had to! She couldn't breathe. The claustrophobic terror tightened

251

around her, suffocating her. In a wild frenzy she pushed rocks aside that under normal circumstances she could never have moved.

Then she heard an ominous growl, and felt a shudder beneath her feet. The rock she had been trying to shove moved of its own accord and some sixth sense sent Trish scrambling to safety only moments before the jumble shifted and moved, spilling more rock into the tunnel. More chunks broke loose from the ceiling and crashed to the floor. Trish fled in wild retreat down one of the smaller tubes.

She ran until she was exhausted, her throat, chest, and sides aching. Finally she slumped to the rough floor of the tunnel, too stunned with shock and terror even to cry. She was trapped. Trapped. No way in or out. No one knew she was here, no one except Edith and Armando and they thought . . . hoped she was already dead.

Why wasn't she? The force of the explosion Armando had set off had thrown her against the wall of the tunnel but she had evidently been far enough away so that the death-rain of broken rock had missed her.

A drop of blood splashed from her cheek to her hand. Vaguely she realized that she had somehow grabbed the flashlight before the grinding rock destroyed it. Now its beam of light seemed all that held back some evil force that was all around her, pressing in and down on her. Carefully clenching the flashlight between her knees, she searched her pockets for something to stop the steady drip of blood from the gash on her cheek. There was a lump on her head too, she noted almost impersonally. It was tender but not bleeding.

She sat there, pressing a handkerchief against the gash, her stunned mind beginning to come to life as she thought how easily Edith and Armando had tricked her, how naively gullible and cooperative she had been. It had been a busy night for them, she reflected bitterly: writing the note, planning the phony little scene to announce Robert Hepler's disappearance; getting the explosives and gun packed and ready in the pickup. And then Trish herself had conveniently suggested the very place they had already planned as her death site. They must have decided they had no time to waste now that Trish knew Edith's father was also her real father. They had to work fast before she also found out about the will, or before she went to Marc and he realized the danger she was in, even if she was too stupid to realize it herself. Stupid, she berated herself wildly. Suspecting first Edith's father, then Marc . . . never having so much as a doubt or suspicion of Armando or Edith.

Oh, yes, she could figure it all out now, see

253

people for what they really were. But it was too late to matter now, far, far too late. Too late to tell Marc she was wrong, too late to tell him she loved him. The image of his lean, aristocratic face seemed to mock her for her errors.

Why think about all that now? she thought despairingly. It did no good to figure out how she had been deceived. Then another shuddering thought hit her: the realization that she had nothing else to do but think, reflect, and regret. Nothing else to do for the rest of her life!

She struggled to her feet again before that thought could deaden her mind and body, and send her into catatonic numbness. She had to keep moving, searching for a way out. There might be something – an animal's burrow, a water-eroded hole – something!

She stumbled on, not knowing which way she was going, wandering from tunnel to tunnel, finding side tunnels and dead ends and strange cavernlike enlargements where the ceiling expanded to shadowy heights above her head. Once she stopped short, hope surging wildly. There was a footprint! Someone had been here. There was another way out!

She rushed forward, her heart pounding with hope, only to stop short again in sickening despair.

The footprint was her own, left there on her search for Robert Hepler, a search that seemed to have taken place eons ago, her footprint like some fossil relic of the past.

She wandered again, her mind wandering too, wondering how Edith felt now that she had won, now that the *cafetal* and Armando were safely, securely hers. No wonder Edith had been so afraid Trish might leave when the first attempts on her life failed, why she had pleaded with Trish to stay. Trish had compassionately attributed this to some fear of rejection on Edith's part, some fear that Trish would abandon her as their mother had once abandoned her. But Edith was afraid only that Trish would escape before they accomplished their goal – killing her! And Armando had so earnestly pleaded that Trish must stay and help him protect Edith from Marc.

How could she have been so wrong, so foolishly wrong, and with such deadly consequences!

Had Edith ever openly admitted to herself that Armando's love and their marriage were based solely on her position as heir to the *cafetal*, the *cafetal* that Armando coveted far more desperately than Marc ever had? If Edith had not admitted the truth to herself, her actions, at least, were based on the subconscious knowledge of what she must do to hold Armando. And perhaps, Trish reflected, Edith did admit the truth to herself. Perhaps her passion for Armando was so great that she simply did not care if having the coffee plantation was necessary to hold him. Whatever the reasons, her passion obviously so obsessed her that she would kill to have him.

Were Edith and Armando even now telling people that Trish had decided to leave? Were they perhaps making a phony trip to San José to pretend to take her to the airport? What would Marc think?

Trish stumbled over something and the flashlight hit the lava wall. The light flickered and for one heart-stopping moment she was in total blackness. Then her frantic shaking and pounding on the flashlight did something and the light came back on.

She slumped against the wall, weak with relief. More than ever, the light was all she had, almost a live thing, protecting her with its magical sphere of illumination. Without it . . . She shivered.

With fresh terror a new realization struck her. Soon the flashlight would go out. Inevitably the batteries would weaken and die. Already she thought she could detect a dimness in the flow, a drawing in of that circle of protection.

She must conserve the light, she thought frantically. Carefully she sat cross-legged on the cold rock and wedged her back into a protective niche in the wall. With trembling hands she switched off the light.

There was darkness – total, hideous darkness beyond anything she had ever known. And silence, a silence she dared not break even with her breathing. Because if she breathed, she might miss some sound, some small hint of something unknown relentlessly hunting her out of the depths of the earth.

She couldn't stand it. Frantically she fumbled with the flashlight switch, and sucked in a breath of air when the reassuring glow lit the walls around her. Unsteadily she stumbled to her feet. She couldn't just sit here, waiting for the terrifying moment when the light flickered and died. She had to keep searching.

She wandered again and found herself back at the starting point, her path blocked by the avalanche of rock. She turned away from the scene of destruction and wandered into another of the smaller tubes. She thought of that very first drive to the coffee plantation with Edith and Armando, the way he had scowled when Edith mentioned this place.

Had he even then had it in mind if his other accidental plans failed?

Armando, the consummate actor. He was wasting his talents on the *cafetal*, Trish thought with a certain wry bitterness. He belonged on the stage. She remembered his convincing surprise at the fire, his self-righteous indignation over the incident with the horse, his earnest explanation of Marc's guilt. The car wreck evidently had been a real accident, but even there Armando had managed to turn the situation to his advantage, to use it to reinforce his accusations against Marc. How cleverly he had turned everything around so it looked as if Marc were guilty!

Marc. She thought of his name, his image, the memory of his kisses, the feel of his lean hard body, and her heart filled with bitter anguish. In those last few moments Armando had said Marc loved her. Was that just another of Armando's lies, his deceptions? But by then there was no more need for deceit. Was it possible Marc did love her?

The possibility that once would have filled her with joy was only an aching pain now, an agony of remorse and regret, of knowing her love for him could never be fulfilled. If only . . .

Her foot hit something and she sprawled

to her knees, the flashlight flying out of her grasp. The beam arced crazily down the length of the lava tube and then snubbed out as the flashlight hit the wall and clattered to the ground. Frantically Trish fumbled for it in the darkness, but all her groping hands found were loose chunks of rocks and the rough, empty floor of the tube. The darkness made her feel dizzy and disoriented, and she had the wild, hysterical feeling that she was crawling on the ceiling, that she was on the edge of falling into some bottomless pit. She searched her pockets frantically for matches, fighting down hysteria, found an old book of them and struck one into a timid flame.

It lasted barely seconds before flickering out, but that was long enough for Trish to spot the flashlight. She felt her way to it in the darkness, only to know final despair and hopelessness when no amount of shaking or pounding would make it work. It was dead. Her moment of terror was here.

She fought the rising hysteria, and fumbled with the matches again. This time she cupped her hand around the little flame, protecting it.

But why, she wondered suddenly, did it need protecting? There was no breeze in here, no fresh air, no opening. And yet when she tentatively removed her cupped hand, the flame distinctly fluttered, as if moved by some slight air current.

Excitedly Trish crept forward in the direction from which the moving air seemed to be coming and struck another match. Yes, there was fresh, moving air here! The flashlight was dead and useless now and she left it behind, using both hands to feel her way along the black tunnel, fighting the apprehensive fear of what her hands might touch in the darkness.

She stopped several times to light matches. Her hands trembled when she realized there was only one match left. One match. Determinedly she saved it, the knowledge that it was there, that she could light it, somehow giving her the strength to keep going.

But she was sure the air current felt distinctly stronger now. The air even seemed to smell fresher, more life-giving. She moved faster, her fingers now moving with eagerness rather than apprehension over the rough walls, her heart pounding with hope.

The tunnel was getting lighter now. Or was it only her imagination, hope playing tricks on her? No, no, it was getting lighter. She looked down at her hands and she could see the outline of her fingers. Air . . . light . . . escape!

She rushed forward, not bothering to feel her way now. She could see the vague shape of the tunnel, though there was no welcome circle of light and freedom at the end, only the vague diffusion of light. Then she rounded a bend and there it was – sunlight!

Sunlight and air and a patch of blue sky overhead. Trish walked dreamlike to where she could stand in the irregular patch of sunlight. She lifted her face to it and closed her eyes and let it warm her body and mind. Sunlight! The tight feeling of claustrophobia loosened, the heavy weight of the mountain lifted. She took a deep, satisfying breath, her mind reacting only to the sensations around her, thinking no farther than this glorious moment of release from the dark terror of the tunnel.

But her feeling of freedom was cruelly short-lived.

At first she thought she must be mistaken. Freedom couldn't be so close and yet so totally unreachable.

The area in which she stood appeared to be a huge bubble of hardened lava. The thin shell overhead had broken through, leaving a large, jagged opening at the top. But the opening was a good twelve or fifteen feet over Trish's head.

She made a rapid tour of the cavernlike area, looking for someplace where she could climb up and reach the opening. The walls were rough and provided hand and footholds but the curve of the overhead bubble prevented her from working her way out to the opening. Twice she climbed as high as she could go, only to have to work her way back to the cavern floor again.

Finally, warm with exertion, she stood with hands on hips and stared up at the jagged opening in frustration. She saw blue sky, even a bird soaring freely overhead, but she was caught here inside the earth, trapped.

The crumbled rock that had fallen from the broken ceiling caught her eye and with a frenzy of energy she started piling the rocks directly below the opening. She worked steadily, even going back into the tunnel to carry chunks of rock to the opening, shoving and turning those that were too heavy to carry. Her fingernails broke and her hands bled, but she worked doggedly, piling the rocks into a steep mound. But when she climbed up to stand on the pile, it was only a pitiful monument to futility. There was still a hopeless expanse of space between her upreaching hands and the opening to freedom. She stood on tiptoe, stretching for every inch, lifting her arms until they ached, but she might as well have been reaching for the moon.

It couldn't be, she thought, dazed.

Freedom couldn't be so tantalizingly close and yet unreachable. But it was.

Finally she had to face what she had so desperately tried to disprove. There was no escape. The opening was there, seductively close, and yet as unreachable as the stars.

The full hopelessness of her situation struck her with dizzying impact. She stumbled down from the pathetic mound of rocks and slumped weakly against the rough wall of the cavern. She was doomed to wait here for a slow death, caught like some trapped animal without food or water. Her wounded hands stung and her head throbbed, but she was conscious only of the final, numbing hopelessness of finding an unattainable freedom, of knowing she had reached a dead end.

Suddenly she tensed. A shadow moved in that jagged opening overhead. A wild animal? No, a person. She could see the silhouette of a head and shoulders now as he peered into the opening. Her mind hadn't even time to register hope before she realized it must be Armando, Armando come to make sure he had done the job right this time, come to finish it if he found her still alive! She shrank against the wall, seeking wildly for escape. Perhaps if she clung to the wall, circled around to the tunnel on the far side

. . . But her flesh crawled at the very thought of fleeing down that dark tube again.

The moment's hesitation cost her the chance to make her escape unnoticed. A rope dangled through the opening and then a lean figure lithely swung hand-over-hand down it. Trish dashed headlong across the cavern before the swinging figure reached the ground.

"Trish!"

The commanding voice stopped her, and she turned, her emotions a strange mixture of fear, hope, and disbelief. It couldn't be . . . but it was!

"Marc!" she breathed.

She stood unmoving at the dark entrance of the tube as he strode toward her. Her eyes took in his tall, powerful figure, the outstretched arms, the chiseled, aristocratic face. But she still wasn't sure what she saw was real and not some wild fantasy until his arms crushed her against him and she felt the lean, solid strength of his body. They didn't speak. Trish felt choked with relief, love, shock, exhaustion, and thirst. Almost numbly she felt his lips on her hair as she pressed her head against his chest, drawing on his strength, surrendering to the security of his embrace. Suddenly he pulled back.

"You're injured! My God . . ." His finger

touched her face gently and came away blood-streaked. He took her hands in his and looked at her raw fingertips. "We've got to get you to a doctor."

"No . . ." Her voice sounded hoarse, as if long disused. "No, I – I'm all right. Just let me rest. I was terrified when I saw you. I thought you were Armando, come back to make sure I was dead."

Marc's hands moved up to grip her shoulders and his dark eyes bore down into hers. "You don't need to fear Armando ever again," he said gently. "He's dead. He miscalculated when he set the explosives and the tunnel came down on top of him."

Too much had happened. Trish couldn't even feel relief. "And Edith?" she asked numbly.

"She's dead too. Buried under the rocks with Armando." His voice was compassionate.

Trish sagged against him, her feelings a mixture of regret, relief, and sadness as what he was telling her slowly sank into her mind. He helped her to the little pile of rocks she had assembled and she sat there. A shiver trembled through her body and Marc sat beside her, his arm tightly protective around her shoulders.

Edith and Armando dead, she thought, caught in their own trap. She thought again of their silhouetted figures, the rocks raining down upon them. She shuddered, and Marc's lips touched her temple.

"How . . . how did you know I was alive?" she asked tremulously.

"I didn't, but I knew I had to look for you. I played around these old tunnels when I was a boy and I remembered this hidden entrance. I'd have been here sooner but I had to go back for the rope."

"But how did you know any of us were here?" She had to have the explanations to make sure she wasn't imagining all this.

"I saw the three of you rush out of the house and leave when I was on my way to the *beneficio*. I thought it odd, but I decided that with everyone gone it would be a good time to see Robert Hepler. For months Edith, Armando, or the nurse stopped me whenever I tried to see him. Even when Edith was injured and I went to see him, the nurse insisted on relaying the message to him herself." He smiled grimly. "But today I decided I would talk to him, nurse or no nurse."

Trish smiled slightly, remembering the determined way he had burst into her bedroom that one morning. No, there was no stopping Marc when he made up his mind. She leaned her head against the secure

266

strength of his shoulder.

"When I saw Señor Hepler, I offered again to buy his property. He said no, that both his daughters were here now and would own the *cafetal* together when he was gone. He seemed very happy and proud. That was when I realized you were in terrible danger and that I had been wrong all along. So I followed the pickup tracks."

"What do you mean, you were wrong?" Trish asked, puzzled. She lifted her head from his shoulder to look into his eyes.

He traced the outline of her lips with his finger. "Wrong about you," he said huskily. "I'd been suspicious of Armando for a long time. I didn't like his absolute power and influence over Edith. I knew how ambitious and greedy he was. Armando came from a family that was once wealthy, with large banana plantation holdings. But they were wiped out by plant disease and poor management. Armando hated working for someone else and was determined to regain his former status. I was afraid for Robert Hepler's safety. I suspected Armando would have no conscience about killing to get the *cafetal*."

Trish nodded slowly.

Marc went on, his voice rueful. "And yet Armando was such a great actor that

267

sometimes he almost convinced even me that he really loved Edith and wasn't marrying her just to get the *cafetal*. But then I heard rumors of a *concubina* in San José, and then you showed up, so much more attractive and desirable than Edith, and I was even more suspicious."

Trish nodded slowly. "I felt you were suspicious of me all the time, but I could never understand why. I still don't," she admitted.

"Because I thought you were working with Armando. I thought you had fallen in love with him when he was in the States and that you had come down here to carry out some scheme with him. That was what I suspected from the very first moment I saw you in the restaurant with Armando and Edith. I feared that Edith as well as her father was in danger then, that you and Armando planned to do away with both of them sooner or later."

"You suspected me of . . . of planning murder?" Trish gasped. "But how could you! I was the one who kept having the strange accidents."

"That puzzled me," he admitted. "I didn't realize what or who was behind those accidents until I talked to Robert Hepler. Then it became clear to me that you were the intended victim."

"And all along I was afraid you were the one causing them," Trish admitted ruefully, remembering that her suspicions had been as totally wrong as those Marc was now admitting. She shook her head regretfully. "We were so suspicious of each other. But you were always so hostile!" she burst out. "And cold and –"

"Hostile, yes," he agreed with a touch of a smile. "But never cold."

"You told me to go away!" she remembered. "You burst right into my bedroom and told me to go home. 'Go home before –' "

He finished the sentence for her now. "Go home before you were so deeply involved in Armando's evil schemes that you couldn't get out. Go away before you helped Armando do something unthinkable."

"And all the time you thought I was in love with Armando," Trish said wonderingly. She looked at him tenderly. "Don't you know what was really happening to me?"

"I knew what was happening to me. I was falling in love with you," he said huskily. "I didn't want to. I tried desperately not to because of my suspicions of your involvement with Armando. That day we went to San José ... do you remember I went to see Hepler's lawyer and ask him to investigate, to see if

269

the lovely blond girl who said she was Patricia Bellingham was really an imposter."

Trish's strength was returning and she straightened indignantly. "You took me to dinner and sight-seeing, and all the time you were investigating me? Of all the . . . the nerve! You kissed me! How could you –"

He silenced her with his lips and Trish felt herself swirling dizzily in the embrace. She was breathless when he finally released her.

"Because, whoever you were, I was falling in love with you," he said simply. "Even if you were in some conspiracy with Armando, I was falling in love with you. Sometimes I thought you were beginning to care for me too. You acted as if you were at the fiesta. That night I tried –"

"Yes, you tried," Trish retorted spiritedly. "Just what was it you were trying to do?"

"To seduce you away from Armando," he admitted. "I thought if I could make you love me I could stop you from getting more deeply embroiled with Armando and his schemes."

"Don't you know you succeeded?" Trish asked softly.

"You rejected me."

"I told you why!"

"And the next day I thought I knew why. I believed you and Armando had planned and almost succeeded in killing Edith in that car wreck," he said grimly. "I didn't know why you were doing it before the wedding, but I was sure the two of you were behind it. Then I knew my attempt to make you fall in love with me had failed."

Trish shook her head regretfully. No wonder he had been so cold and hostile that morning at the hospital. He suspected her of attempted murder! "And I thought you were the one who caused the accident so that with Edith dead you could buy the plantation cheaply from Robert Hepler. Later I even thought you had planned to kill me in the accident too." She paused. "But that time we were both wrong, it appears. The car wreck really was just an accident."

Marc shook his head. "No. I inspected the brake line on the car. It was deliberately broken."

"But who...? Why?" Trish asked, puzzled.

"Armando."

"Armando?" Trish repeated blankly. "But that doesn't make sense. Armando wanted me dead and yet it was he who kept me out of the car that night."

"Yes, but Armando had a momentary change of plans," Marc said grimly. "He decided to kill Edith."

"But that still makes no sense," Trish

271

protested, even more bewildered. "With Edith dead he would have no chance to get the *cafetal*."

"He thought he had. Armando decided he could acquire the *cafetal* just as easily through you as through Edith. You were both Robert Hepler's daughters. And heirs."

"But I still don't understand," Trish protested.

"Don't you?" Marc asked gently. He tilted her chin up with one hand and smoothed her dusty hair with the other. "Didn't you ever take a good look at yourself in the mirror, Trish? Compare yourself with Edith? See how much younger and prettier and more attractive you are? Look at yourself through Armando's greedy, calculating eyes. Do you not think Armando would rather have had you, so beautiful and desirable, to go with his property rather than plain, dowdy Edith?"

"Oh, no," Trish protested again, almost unwilling to accept this fresh evil in Armando's character, to realize how cold-bloodedly he had decided to get rid of Edith after professing his love for her.

"I saw him look at you with his greedy eyes," Marc went on almost bitterly. "Such as the time you came down from the mountain and he saw you there in your torn blouse – though at the time the way he looked at you

272

was only more proof to me that the two of you had some secret . . . relationship."

Yes, Trish thought with a shudder. That night at the fiesta Armando had kissed her hand, kissed it at the very moment Edith's car was in flames, after deliberately provoking a disagreement with her. He had manufactured a reason to keep Trish out of the sabotaged car. And later he had cleverly taken the blame for upsetting Edith and causing the accident, thereby effectively concealing his real crime in tampering with the car's brakes. She remembered, too, how he had cut off that final conversation between himself and Edith in the tunnel when the car wreck was mentioned.

His cold-blooded, evil schemes knew no end. Trish shuddered again, and in spite of what Edith had tried to do to her, Trish found herself hoping Edith had not had time before she died to realize Armando never really loved her, that he had once decided to kill her too.

"Armando, of course, had supreme confidence in his ability to win any woman," Marc added with a hint of contempt in his voice. "I'm sure he had a very pleasant vision of himself as a *cafetal* owner with you as his beautiful wife at his side."

"But he changed his mind about me," Trish said slowly.

Marc nodded. "Evidently so. When Edith survived the accident, he decided to go back to his original plan and get rid of you. It was safer. He was sure of his ability to control Edith and make her do whatever he wanted. You might be more desirable, but you were also more risky, more independent, less controllable. He knew Edith was so desperately in love with him that she would do anything for him."

They were both silent then, thinking of Edith's love and what it had cost her. Trish realized suddenly how little she had really known her sister, so quiet and reserved on the surface, so seething with passion underneath. How little anyone had really known her, except perhaps Armando. Edith had played her part well too, Trish thought with a pang, remembering all the times Edith had deceived her. All for love of Armando.

"All that love," Trish said regretfully. "Wasted on a man such as Armando."

Marc nodded. "Yes," he said. His voice suddenly sounded aloof and impersonal. "Love is sometimes a mistake." He stood up almost abruptly. "Think you can climb out now?"

Trish looked up at him, surprised and dismayed by his sudden change of demeanor. "I'll try," she said uncertainly.

She stood on top of the pile of rocks she had collected and grasped the rope tentatively, remembering how long ago she used to shinny up a rope-swing at home, never dreaming it might someday mean her survival. She took a firm grip on the rope and started up. Marc boosted her as far as he could reach and then she was on her own, painfully aware of the rough rope against the rawness of her hands as she worked her way toward that jagged patch of blue sky. She paused to catch her breath just before she reached the opening, wrapping a loop of rope around her foot to support her weight.

Marc was standing down below, looking up at her. From up above, his face looked shadowy in the depths of the dusky cavern, shadowy and faraway. She had felt so close to him in his arms, but suddenly she realized he had said several times that he was falling in love with her. But never that he was in love with her now.

He had also said he had fought against that love. He had fought against it and won ... because now there was Ramona! Trish remembered with an aching heart how Ramona had looked that night in Marc's home, how his arm had tightened around her as she stood next to him, so lovely in her revealing peignoir. Marc had conquered the love he did not want to feel for Trish and found fulfillment in Ramona's arms. And in those final words he had told Trish the sad truth: Some loves were a mistake.

"Is something wrong?" he called out sharply.

Wrong, she thought wildly. Only that she had momentarily glimpsed the wonders of Marc's love in the same way she had glimpsed the jagged opening to freedom, as a wondrous, desirable thing. But hopelessly unattainable.

But all she said was a curt, "Sorry, I was just resting a minute," before she scrambled out of the hole and into the bright sunlight. Once outside, she glanced around, seeing nothing familiar except the menacing hulk of Monte Decepción looming over her. The hole in the ground here was practically unnoticeable among the misshapen rocks and stunted vegetation. A ridge of rock separated it from the main entrance.

A moment later Marc swung his lean body up beside her. Swiftly and efficiently he untied the rope from a nearby rock and looped it into neat coils.

"The pickup is over that way," he said, jerking his head toward the rocky ridge. "We're going to have to break the news to Robert Hepler."

Trish started off, her head held high with

hurt pride at his suddenly impersonal attitude. Through all the day's ordeal, through all the terror and pain, no tears had dampened her eyes, but now she felt them trickling down her cheeks, blinding her. Carefully she kept her face turned away from Marc, aware that he was following her only by an occasional rustle or crunch of rock.

She blinked, trying to stop the tears, but they wouldn't go away. She was concentrating so hard on not letting Marc know she was crying that she tripped over a rock and stumbled almost to her knees before his strong hand caught and straightened her.

She looked up at him defiantly, aware that she must be a strange sight with a cut face, tear-streaked cheeks, and disheveled hair. She jerked her arm free of his grasp.

"You're crying," he observed. He reached out to brush a tangle of hair from her eyes, but she pulled away again.

"Why didn't you just leave me there to die?" she cried in sudden anguish.

"Don't be a fool," he said curtly.

"Yes, yes, I'm a fool!" she cried wildly, tears streaming unheeded down her cheeks now. "Because I'm in love with you!"

He regarded her coolly, but a muscle twitched along his lean jawline. "And what will you think if I tell you now that I am also in love with you?"

Trish stared at him. He was saying he was in love with her and yet his cold eyes and hard face hardly matched his words. He looked down at her, waiting, and slowly Trish's mind went over the situation and all that had happened. She was Robert Hepler's only daughter now and someday the *cafetal* would be hers, the *cafetal* Marc had long tried to possess.

"You see?" he said harshly, as the realization dawned on her face. "If I tell you I love you now, you will think I want you only because you will someday inherit the coffee plantation. I love you. But I would never want that suspicion to come between us."

"And Ramona?" Trish asked slowly.

"Ramona." Marc repeated the name carelessly, without emotion. He shrugged. "I wanted to love her. I brought her out to the house hoping I could forget you in her arms. But it didn't work. I couldn't even force myself to touch her. Because I was in love with you. In spite of all the terrible things I believed about you, I was in love with you. I still am," he added almost angrily.

"Someday," Trish began with a tremulous smile, "someday I'll tell you all the awful things I believed about you."

He reached out and caught her by the

278

shoulders. His eyes were unfathomable now, but they held hers like a magnet. "Can you believe I love you? That I don't give a damn about the *cafetal*?" he asked roughly. "That I want to marry you only because I love you?"

The coffee plantation meant nothing to Trish. Only Marc's love mattered. But she knew his fierce pride.

"We'll make a bargain," she said shakily. "If . . . if this half of the *cafetal* ever does become mine, it will always be mine. Then I will never have to suspect you married me for it."

"Agreed," he said simply. He looked down at her and she lifted her mouth for his kiss. His dark eyes, reflecting nothing of her dirt-streaked face or disheveled hair, revealed only the depths of his love. His lips found hers then in a kiss of passion and tenderness that left no doubt in Trish's heart of his true feelings.

But somewhere far back in her mind another thought danced. Part of the *cafetal* might always be hers alone, but someday it would all be one again, as it should be, through their children. And then she gave herself up to the wonder and passion of his kiss and all it promised.

The publishers hope that this book has given you enjoyable reading. Large Print Books are specially designed to be as easy to see and hold as possible. If you wish a complete list of our books, please ask at your local library or write directly to: Curley Publishing, Inc., P.O. Box 37, South Yarmouth, Massachusetts, 02664.